1. Ned Harrison Arkle-Smith is like no other character you've met before.

2. You'll discover what wallboggling is!

3. A story of family, friends, mystery, and magic.

4. Perfect for fans of Ross Welford.

5. A fresh and unique story by a truly talented writer.

## Meet Ned Harrison Arkle-Smith . . .

I knew straight off I'd been sleepwalking. That my sleepwalking self had expected a big landing to sleepwalk along—and NOT a small lobby. Not all the new walls.

I could hear noises from downstairs—the TV. Some kind of noisy game show, with the audience laughing and laughing.

I was NOT laughing. I was furious. And in pain. My head was throbbing. Really throbbing . . .

And the thing about the pain is—it made me want to blame someone. Someone . . . or something.

So I glared at the wall, the dad-wall—and then I started talking to it. 'It was you,' I said, glaring. 'See this lump on my head? You did that. YOU!'

Look—I'm just telling you what happened. I'm not saying it makes sense. Not now. But it did at the time. Maybe I was concussed. Maybe I wasn't. Who knows? But whatever I was, I started to give the wall a good kicking.

'You're in the way,' I told it. 'Go and be a wall somewhere else. NOT HERE.'

Then, when the wall didn't reply, I just got angrier. 'Not talking?' I said. 'NOT TALKING?' And I kicked at it—hard—with my feet.

I stood there, in the lobby. Full of anger. HATING the walls. Hating every single wall I could see.

Because I had just realized something.

That—all this time, ever since that day Mum and Dad first told us they were splitting up—I had never given up hope. Hope that Mum and Dad would change their minds. That one day they'd STOP being split up and get back together.

But now I knew.

This lobby, the walls, all the walls—they were PROOF.

Mum, Dad... They would never change their minds. Never knock down the walls. It was just not going to happen.

Not EVER.

So I started kicking the wall more.

'You're a stupid wall,' I said, kicking it harder and harder. 'An EVIL wall. You're wrong, wrong, WRONG. You should NOT be here.'

Now I started pummelling the wall with my fists. Pummelling hard as I could. Kicking harder with my feet. Kicking and kicking and kicking—I could NOT stop kicking.

I felt that, if a boy could reach boiling point like water does—then I'd just reached it.

'I hate you,' I told the wall. 'Hate you. Hate you. HATE you.'

My eyes felt burning hot now. So did the rest of me. I felt blazing. Sizzling. Like I was bubbling and boiling, and on fire. Then a feeling whooshed right through me. Like a gigantic surge of POWER. Of ENERGY...

And that is when it happened.

When my pummelling fists, my kicking foot, went straight through the wall. Straight through it—as if it JUST WASN'T THERE.

I gaped. I rubbed my eyes. Stared at the wall. My fists... My foot... How did they do that?

It was impossible.

IMPOSSIBLE.

But it had just happened.

And then, standing there, staring, a thought thrilled right through me...

If my fists can go straight through that wall, and so can my foot—then, maybe, so can the REST of me.

# OXFORD
## UNIVERSITY PRESS

Great Clarendon Street, Oxford OX2 6DP

Oxford University Press is a department of the University of Oxford.
It furthers the University's objective of excellence in research, scholarship,
and education by publishing worldwide. Oxford is a registered trade mark of
Oxford University Press in the UK and in certain other countries

British Library Cataloguing in Publication Data
Data available

ISBN: 978-0-19-276382-2

1 3 5 7 9 10 8 6 4 2

Printed in Great Britain

Paper used in the production of this book is a natural,
recyclable product made from wood grown in sustainable forests.
The manufacturing process conforms to the environmental
regulations of the country of origin.

# Emma Fischel

# WALLS

OXFORD
UNIVERSITY PRESS

*For Theo and Iris*

'A wall?' I said, and I gaped—first at Mum, then at Dad. 'A *wall*? You are planning to build a WALL, right down the middle of Ivy Lodge? Right down the middle of my HOME?'

I sat there, at the kitchen table, head spinning. Feeling shocked, helpless, at what I'd just heard. At what Mum and Dad had just told us.

The wall...

What a terrible TERRIBLE thing. Splitting the house. Splitting it in two. By building a wall right down the middle.

A wall with Mum living one side of it, and Dad the other. And us kids—me and the sisters—spending one week the mum-side, the next week the dad-side.

No. No, no, *no*.

The *first* thing Mum and Dad told us—that was bad enough. The thing last year. When Mum and Dad sat us all down, then told us this...

That they were splitting up. NOT planning to be our mum and dad together any more, but separately.

That Dad was going to rent a house down in town—number 3, Columbus Road. That we were staying here, in Ivy Lodge, with Mum.

That it was nothing we'd done, and we'd still see Dad lots.

But now THIS—this *second* thing, it was just as bad.

I sat there, trying to speak. But I couldn't.

Because now Mum and Dad were telling us why splitting Ivy Lodge was a *good* plan. A cheaper plan. A better plan. That this way Dad could stop spending so much money on rent.

It was not a better plan.

Mum and Dad could *not* do this. Could NOT split Ivy Lodge, so big, so old, so full of history. Shabby and creaky—and perfect. *Perfect.* Just the way it was.

And now the sisters were speaking. I could hear both of them, both speaking, both asking questions. Lots of questions.

But not me.

Nothing came out of my mouth. Only splutters and buts.

'But... but...' I could hear myself going. 'But...'

So I gave up. Just sat there, shaking my head, while my insides did somersaults, again and again.

Mum... Dad... The wall... it could *not* happen.

But it did.

It took ALL SUMMER LONG to turn one fat house into two skinny ones. From the start of the summer term, right up to the end of the holidays.

Because it wasn't just the one new wall Ivy Lodge turned out to need. It was *lots* of new walls. But first there had to be drawings of where all the new walls would be. And the people in charge of new walls kept wanting changes to the drawings. Then, when the drawings were—*finally*—right, we had to move out.

Me, Mum and the sisters went away all summer long, the whole of the holidays. But now all the wall-building was finished. And today, Sunday—*at last*—we were back.

Back...

I stared out of the car window as we turned into the driveway.

I stared and I stared.

There it was. Ivy Lodge. The house I had been missing all summer.

From the outside, Ivy Lodge looked just the same. Big and square and solid-looking. Same yellow front door. Same gardens all round. Same swing hanging off the same branch of the same tree.

It was a *trick*.

Mum opened the front door—and inside it was NOT the same.

It was the walls. The new walls. New walls—*everywhere*. Starting right here, just inside the front door.

I stood there, stunned. Thoughts smashing and crashing and colliding in my brain. My mind was boggled. Utterly BOGGLED.

Because Ivy Lodge—it was a mind-boggling sight.

But not *good* mind-boggling. Not astonishing, amazing, brilliant mind-boggling—like seeing the Northern Lights, or Niagara Falls, or the Great Pyramid of Giza.

No.

*Bad* mind-boggling. Mind-boggling so bad I thought I might actually be sick.

This was NOT home. Not *my* home. Not any more.

Because the big old hallway, with the wide wooden staircase sweeping right up the middle—it was *gone*.

In its place...

Walls.

A wall behind me, with the front door in it. A wall ahead of me—a few steps away. And walls either side of me. Both with new doors...

A mum-door to the left. A dad-door to the right.

The *lobby*, Mum called this place.

But... this lobby, it couldn't be real. It *couldn't*.

This was a dream. HAD to be. Any minute now, I'd wake up—and this *whole year* would turn out to be a dream.

I crossed my fingers, tight as I could.

Please, please let this be a dream. Let me wake up and find Mum and Dad still together. And Ivy Lodge just how it was. With no new walls, and no new lobby.

But—this *wasn't* a dream. This was actually happening.

Now Mum was putting a key in the lock of the mum-door. And in we went, through the mum-door, to find— guess what?

MORE walls.

Walls everywhere.

And rooms. New rooms, smaller rooms. Different rooms.

It was all wrong. Wrong, wrong, WRONG.

I knew the walls would be there—Dad showed me

all the drawings. But seeing the walls on drawings was NOT the same as seeing the walls in real life.

They changed *everything*, all those walls. Where rooms were—*what* rooms were. Nothing looked right. Nothing looked like home. Nothing *felt* like home.

The sisters didn't seem to mind all the new walls. They seemed happy to be back. To be home. They charged from room to room, oohing and aahing. Seemed excited. Interested. Almost *pleased*. And even more pleased when Dad turned up, and showed us round the dad-side.

*Not* me.

'Ned,' said Mum, back in the mum-kitchen. 'What do you think?'

I turned and glared at her.

'What do I think?' I said. 'I think you and Dad are IDIOTS. I *hate* every single new wall. And I am now going out.'

Then I stuck my nose right in the air—to make one hundred per cent *sure* Mum understood how I was feeling.

'I am going to Bill's house...' I said, 'where all the walls are in the RIGHT PLACE.'

Bill...William James Egg...My very best friend—since the first day of term, one whole year ago.

I remember how I felt that day. Gloomy. Fed up. And miserable.

It was five days—five *monstrous* days—since Mum and Dad had told us they were splitting up. How things were changing. How Dad was moving out.

Five days of me trying to force Mum and Dad to change their minds. Trying and trying. But failing.

So I trudged into the classroom, and sat down at my new table. A two-seater, with my name on it, and another name...

**WILLIAM JAMES EGG**

Oh. A new boy.

Was I pleased? Not pleased? I had no idea. My brain felt full up. Full up with Mum and Dad's plans—for them and for us. Too full up for any thinking about the new boy.

So I sorted my pencils instead. Put them in colour order, darkest to lightest. Then I lined them up on the table—in the straightest, neatest line I could.

I stared down, scowling. Wishing and *wishing* I could sort Mum and Dad the way I had sorted my pencils. But knowing I couldn't.

Then the classroom door opened, and there was the new boy. My height, scruffy hair, a sprinkling of freckles—and a big stretchy grin right across his face.

Miss Blake, our teacher, brought him over. 'Ned,' she said. 'This is Bill. And this is for you.'

Then she handed me something round and blue…

The buddy badge!

I pinned it on, feeling proud. Because a kid with the buddy badge is in charge. Takes care of a new kid for the first few days. Shows them around. Answers their questions.

Bill sat down. He looked at me, then down at my pencils, then back at me. He beamed. A beam so big, so cheery—it made me start beaming myself. And straight off, I felt less miserable.

'Oh, that's excellent,' he said, unzipping his pencil case. 'I'm doing that too.'

He got out all his pencils. Sorted them into colour order, darkest to lightest, then lined them up carefully—just the way I'd done mine.

And that was it. Me and Bill were friends from then on.

I buddied him all day long. Told him what to do and how to do it. And Bill did it.

Happiness surged through me. Because Bill—unlike Mum and Dad—*wanted* me to sort him out. He wanted to listen. Wanted to do EXACTLY what I said.

It was the same the next day, and the day after that. And by the time I stopped wearing the buddy badge it had become … well, sort of a *habit*. Me telling Bill what to think, what to do. Bill doing it.

And that's how things have been all year long. Me and Bill—a brilliant team.

I ran. I ran fast as I could. I had to see Bill, and *now*.

Because I had just had SIX WHOLE WEEKS without Bill. And, even though school started tomorrow—tomorrow was just *too long* to wait.

So I ran. Pounded out of the Ivy Lodge front gates, left down the road, then through the gate to the footpath.

I raced along the footpath, high on the hills above Craggelton. Big fields stretched away to one side of me. And there, below me, was the town—all bright painted houses and steep narrow streets, winding up and away from the sea.

On and on I ran. Past the little clump of trees all crouching the same way, bent and blasted by gales blowing in from the sea. Past the brick shelter, with its seats inside. On to the end of the footpath, and the gate.

The gate whined and complained, like it always does, as I opened it. And there it was—Bill's street! The last street in Craggelton, steepest of all, and backing on to the cliffs. With Bill's house—smallish, lots of windows, and not old at all—tucked away near the top.

And here came Bill. *Bill!* Bursting out of his front door. Jumping up and down, and waving at me.

'Bill!' I yelled, hurtling down the street towards him. 'Bill!'

'Ned,' Bill yelled back, beaming his great big Bill-beam and flinging open his front gate. 'Ned!'

Then we collided.

We did our secret seven-part handshake. Starting with a punch to the left shoulder. Ending with a slap to the right knee.

Except Bill *didn't* end there. Because after the slap

to the knee, Bill twirled round. He did one whole extra twirl.

I stared at him. 'What are you doing?' I said.

'I added it,' said Bill, sounding proud. 'I was thinking—we could make it an eight-parter. Or even nine!'

I was shocked. Bill thinking! Wanting to change our secret seven-part handshake!

'Bill,' I said, firmly. 'I think it's fine as it is. A seven-parter. No need to change it.'

Bill's shoulders slumped. He gave a sigh. 'OK,' he said. 'We'll keep it your way.'

I stared. Why were Bill's shoulders slumping? Why was he sighing? What was there to sigh about?

I started to feel uneasy. Had six weeks apart got Bill confused? Had he forgotten how our friendship worked?

Never mind. I was back now. He'd soon remember.

Bill's mum and dad were in the kitchen, having the sort of talk mums and dads *should* have. About gardening— and NOT about walls.

They asked me about my summer, so I told them the truth. That it was rubbish. That I missed Bill. That I was glad to be back.

Then I pushed Bill towards the stairs, and we shot up to his bedroom.

We call Bill's bedroom the Tower because it's perched at the top of the house, with windows on three sides, like a lookout tower. Then we squashed ourselves in his swinging chair, which hangs down from the ceiling. And...

'I declare this meeting of the Tower Two open!' I said.

The Tower Two is our secret society. And we have meetings where we do secret stuff. So far, the Tower Two have done the following secret stuff:

- Invented a secret language.
- Invented a secret code for messages.
- Built secret pockets in our socks.
- Worn secret disguises to walk through Craggelton.
- Left secret trails for each other, using twigs and pebbles.

But now Bill was sitting there with a dreamy sort of look on his face.

I stared. I felt my eyes narrow. It looked suspiciously as if Bill was doing more thinking.

He was.

'I was thinking, over the summer,' Bill said. 'Maybe some other kids could join the Tower Two.'

'Bill,' I said, shaking my head. 'You are confused. Because if other kids joined the Tower Two we wouldn't *be* the Tower Two.'

'No,' said Bill, and his eyebrows were knotted—with the effort of all his thinking. 'I know that. But we could be the Tower Three. Or the Tower Four.'

I was feeling more and more uneasy. And a bit annoyed with Bill. *Obviously* we didn't need other kids to join the Tower Two. Why was Bill thinking something so strange?

'The whole point of this being a secret society is that we keep it SECRET,' I explained—slowly, to make sure Bill understood. 'And if we tell any other kids about it, then it's NOT secret.'

Then I told him my plan for the Tower Two meeting. 'Today,' I said, 'the secret stuff we are doing is this. Searching the caves for the secret wreckers' tunnel!'

**3**

Bill's road winds steeply down from the cliffs. Down and down and down, all the way to the seafront, and Craggelton beach, where the caves are.

But as soon as me and Bill set off I spotted a shadowy figure, crouched behind a tree further down the road…

Waiting.

Snapper—otherwise known as Samuel Snare.

'Bill!' I said, grabbing his arm. 'Snapper alert!'

Too late. Snapper had spotted us. Out he leapt from behind the tree, and came charging up the road towards us.

We ran. Ducked down the side alley by Bill's, swerved into Cross Street, and took the first right turn we could.

Snapper has lived in Craggelton—near the bottom of Bill's road—as long as I have. And for years now, he's been pranking me. Ambushing me, squirting cream in my face, tripping me up, dropping water bombs on my head from trees...

But lately he's changed. Gone from being a nuisance, a pest, like an annoying buzzy wasp you can't get rid of—to something worse. Something meaner. Something nastier.

He's shifty and sneaky. He punches and shoves. He kicks, and does angry stuff. Bullying stuff. Stuff that *hurts*.

And he does it to Bill too—any time he spots him coming out of his house.

I could hear Snapper now, yelling behind us. 'Ned!' he yelled. 'Neddy boy. Bill! Wait for meeee!'

'Keep running,' I panted, ducking and swerving my way through the maze of back streets in Craggelton, Bill by my side.

But Snapper was hard to lose. He's wiry and strong—and whippet-fast. And I could *still* hear him yelling after us.

'Faster,' I said to Bill. 'FASTER!'

I thought we'd *never* get rid of him. But we did eventually. His yells tailed off and I stopped in Salt Street, right by the seafront, gasping for breath.

'I think we lost him,' I panted. Then, cautiously, I stuck my head round the corner. Stared right, then left, all along the promenade. Checking, double-checking.

No sign of Snapper. He was gone... for now.

\* \* \*

I stood on the seafront, staring at the sea—glistening and gleaming, with little waves breaking far out on the sand. I took big sniffs of the salty air.

The sea… the beach… I had missed it all summer.

It's a big beach, Craggelton beach. Curving and sandy, with cliffs towering up at each end. And there are rocks, big lumpy rocks piled up at the far end of the beach. Rocks spilling over the sand and right out to sea.

That's where the caves are—beyond the rocks.

At low tide, like now, the sea goes right out, and you can walk round the rocks from the beach to the caves. But me and Bill never bother. Because the rocks are brilliant for climbing. So that's the way we always go.

We did today. We ran across the beach, scrambled to the top of the rocks, then down the other side. And there were the caves.

We hopped down from the rocks, then across the soggy sand. Past the big notice…

**CAUTION!**
**CHECK TIDE TIMES!**
**DON'T GET CUT OFF BY INCOMING TIDE!**

Me and Bill know to check the tide times. Because this bit of beach disappears when the tide comes in. It gets swallowed up by the sea. And all the caves get swamped with water.

But not now. Not for a few hours yet. So me and Bill went into the caves. One main cave, not that tall, but wide—with four smaller caves off it. Damp, drippy sort of caves.

When I first decided me and Bill were being a secret society, I thought the caves would be a good meeting place. And that we could call ourselves the Champion Cavers.

But then I realized something. It was no good planning meetings for every Saturday afternoon when some Saturday afternoons the cave would be underwater. That's how we ended up the Tower Two instead.

They're strange-looking caves, the Craggelton caves. All old and wrinkly looking. With lots of lines in the rock, like ridges.

Dad told me the ridges are called striations. Lots and lots of striations, formed over thousands of years. Going up and down and along the rocks.

And somewhere in the caves there's supposed to be a tunnel. A secret tunnel with a hidden entrance. A tunnel built by wreckers, leading from the caves up to the cliffs.

Because back in the olden days, lots of ships got wrecked at low tide—dashed to pieces on the rocks around Craggelton Bay. And wreckers would rush to plunder and loot them.

But the wreckers got in BIG TROUBLE if they were caught. So rumour has it they built a tunnel from the beach to the cliffs. A way to get their loot hidden, fast as they could.

No one's ever found the tunnel though.

Not YET.

But maybe today—the Tower Two would *succeed.*

The Tower Two didn't. Me and Bill searched the caves—looking around the main cave first, then the smaller ones. Not a sign of the secret wreckers' tunnel. No hidden entrance—nothing. Not anywhere.

And it was getting a bit boring looking for a secret wreckers' tunnel—so I had another idea.

I led Bill back into the main cave. 'Let's carve a secret message,' I said. 'On that bit of wall.'

Because there's one bit in the main cave that doesn't have too many striations. Hardly any ridges or wrinkles. A smoothish bit. Perfect for a secret message.

I got out my code wheel—made by following instructions from *Secret Sleuth*, number one of my top ten favourite books—and sorted us a code. Then I found a sharp bit of rock, and me and Bill got carving, doing letters in turn...

## MAX MHPXK MPH YHK XOXK!

'There,' I said. 'The Tower Two for ever!'

'The Tower Two for ever!' beamed Bill, and we did our secret handshake and left the cave.

Then I heard a noise. A cracking, slithering noise, high above us.

I looked up. A small chunk of rock was tumbling down. Down and down—heading straight towards Bill. And Bill was just standing there, staring up at it. Goggle-eyed, not moving.

'Bill! Watch out!' I shouted, then I hurled myself at him. I pushed him to one side, just as—SMASH!—the rock hit the sand.

Bill stared down. Then he stared at me. Gave me the sort of look a boy would give a superhero. 'I think you just saved my actual LIFE,' he said.

I nodded proudly. 'I think I just did,' I said. Then I looked down at the rock—and my insides gave a lurch just thinking of what that rock might have done to Bill. A big BIG lurch...

And that was my first lurch of the day—but *not* the last.

Because I looked up at the clifftop—and straight off, I got ANOTHER lurch.

Someone was up there. Someone broad and burly, staring down at us.

The Hulk...

Well, that's what me and Bill call him. He's maybe four years older than us. Big and tough and strong-looking.

He's been in town the last few months, smirking and swaggering his way around. But he never bothers us, not like Snapper does.

Although, as that big burly figure swaggered off, for a moment I wondered... Did that rock fall by itself? Or did it not?

And that was NOT the end of the lurches. Because on the way home, I stopped off at my secret spot. And I got my THIRD lurch of the day.

My secret spot is on the riverbank, over the wall at the bottom of the Ivy Lodge garden. Because the river Daunt runs behind Ivy Lodge, then on through Craggelton and down to the bay.

It's not a big deep river, the Daunt—not near Ivy Lodge anyway. It's shallow, and busy, and fast-moving. And my secret spot is a bit of flat riverbank, with a pebbly beach and big boulders scattered about—just right for a kid to jump about on, or sit on.

It's got long views, my secret spot, across the hills to the sea. And it's peaceful, because no one else uses it. Not the sisters, and not Vine Cottage next door.

Vine Cottage also has a wall backing on to the riverbank. But Vine Cottage has been empty for over a year. And before that, Mrs Diggle lived there, who was much too old to climb walls. Especially high ones, like this one.

So, as soon as I got home, I ran through the side gate and down the garden. I scrambled my way up the wall, and over the top. Then jumped off and slithered down the bank to my secret spot.

And that's when I got the third lurch.

There was someone there. Sitting right on my FAVOURITE boulder, reading a book. A girl with corkscrew curls and big clompy boots...

I stared, shocked. Who was that girl? What was she doing here? At my secret spot?

Whoever she was, she turned, and stared back at me. She had scary eyes—the shape of almonds, the colour of conkers. And glinty. *Very* glinty.

I glared at her. 'You're trespassing,' I said.

She glared too. '*You're* trespassing,' she said.

I scowled and narrowed my eyes. She scowled and narrowed hers. 'I live here and this is MY secret spot,' I said.

'I live here too,' she said. 'There.' And she pointed over the wall.

Oh no. Oh no no *no*. Vine Cottage... She must have moved in.

I'd been hoping and hoping a kid would move in. A kid my age. But not a girl—I've got sisters, that's enough girls. And definitely not THIS girl. All scowly and glinting, with a pointy sharp face.

'And how is it secret?' she said, glinting more. '*I* found it. Easily. A secret spot should be one no other kids can find. ANY kid could find this, just like I did. So it's just a *spot*—not a secret spot.'

'But... I was here FIRST,' I said. 'I made a den and everything.'

Which I have. Just a bit further along the riverbank, in the bushes.

'Saw it,' she said. 'Not much of a den. Could do a LOT better.'

Then she stood up. And standing, she was WAY taller than me—towering over me in her big clompy boots.

She snapped her book shut and shoved it in her bag, but I saw the title and—oh no—I got my FOURTH lurch of the day.

She had *Secret Sleuth*—the OMNIBUS edition. All six *Secret Sleuth* books in one big fat book.

I felt my teeth grind. I only have two of the *Secret Sleuth* books—*Tracking and Trailing*, and *Surprises and Disguises*. She had the WHOLE LOT. It was not *fair*. So I scowled at her.

She scowled back. 'Next time,' she said, 'look before you leap.'

Then she pointed at a bag on the ground behind me. 'See that?' she said. 'That used to be a panini until you squashed it.'

She picked up the flattened bag and with one last scowl, she was gone. Scrambling up her own bit of wall and into the Vine Cottage garden.

**4**

The lurches were *still* not over. Because later that evening I decided to watch TV—and I got my FIFTH lurch of the day.

It was because of the hairy beanbag.

I always *always* watch TV sitting on the hairy beanbag. It's big, it's dark red, and it's covered in long fluffy hair. It's very soft, and I can sink right into it—BUT...

It was not here. Because it was in the dad-side.

I tried to watch TV *not* sitting on the hairy beanbag. I sat in the armchair, but it was all wrong. So was the sofa. It HAD to be the hairy beanbag.

And even though I was watching a documentary about Madagascar—the best, most interesting island in the whole world—I could NOT concentrate.

So I stomped off to bed in a very bad mood. And when I slept, my dreams were all about walls. Walls—blocking my way, walls stopping me from getting where I wanted to go.

Then I woke up. Or, rather, *someone* woke me up ...

'If a witch on a broomstick flied as fast as she could, and so did a dragon,' bellowed a voice—high-pitched and piercing—straight into my ear, 'who would be winner?'

I groaned, and opened my eyes. And there she was.

Isabel. My sister. Four years old. Small and chunky. With a solemn face, round as a moon, and snow-white hair pulled into pigtails. Dressed as an elf—all in green, with pointy red boots and a pointy red hat with a tinkling bell.

Isabel folded her arms. She started tapping one pointy boot, hat wobbling, bell tinkling. 'What is the answer? Who would be winner?' she said.

I groaned again.

That's how most of my mornings start. Isabel and her questions. And the questions go on all day long ...

- **'If I see a fairy will it die?'**
- **'Do witches bleed red or green blood?'**
- **'Do trolls eat biscuits?'**

On and on and ON.

Isabel frowned. 'I am *still* waiting for my answer,' she

said—sternly, and with more of the foot tapping. 'And I have been waiting a LONG time.'

I heaved a sigh.

I knew Isabel. She'd just stand there, staring at me with her big round eyes—bright-blue and unblinking—until she got some kind of reply. It's scary how long Isabel can go without blinking those eyes of hers.

I *had* to get rid of her. So I did, the only way I could.

'Dragon,' I said. 'Flies forty-seven miles an hour, top speed. Fastest broomstick only ever managed thirty-three. Now go away.'

Then I pulled the duvet back over my head. Miserable.

Because here, in my bedroom, things were the same. Same room. Same things. Nothing was changed.

Which meant that—just for a moment, just for a second when Isabel first woke me—my bedroom had fooled me. Made me think Ivy Lodge was the same. That nothing had changed.

But it had. It *had*.


I headed out of my room and on to the landing, the top floor landing.

The top floor—the attic floor—is where me and

the sisters all sleep. It has no new walls. It's just how it always was.

I headed past Isabel's door, wide open. Past Grace's door, tight shut. And down the stairs...

The stairs, and the changes. Because it's down the attic stairs the changes begin. The changes—and all the new walls.

I sat on the bottom step and glared around me.

The bottom step was my favourite place to sit in the whole of Ivy Lodge. With the whole first floor landing spread out in front of me. Stairs winding up from the hallway. Doors off left and right.

And, best of all, big windows, two of them, at the far end—with big BIG views of the rolling hills. And the sparkling sea in the distance.

But now? *Ruined.*

Because sitting here, on the bottom step—the landing, the views, they were GONE.

In their place—*another* lobby. Another small room, just like downstairs. With a wall straight ahead. Walls either side. And two new doors.

The mum-door, which was open. And the dad-door, which was locked.

And that, according to Mum and Dad, is the genius part of their plan. No big move for us kids each week. Just a different door open, and a different door locked.

So I sat there, feeling glum, staring at the wall straight ahead. At the big painting on it. A portrait, one that used to be on the landing wall, of an olden-days relative.

A woman with a fierce mouth, a strong nose, and staring eyes. Wearing a long dark dress and weird shoes. Standing in a gloomy room, with a big globe on a table beside her.

Matilda Arkle, her name was.

Mum has told me about her. How Matilda Arkle was born over one hundred and fifty years ago. Back when most women stayed at home, sewing, and flower arranging, and dusting things. But *not* Matilda Arkle. She was an explorer. She went travelling all over the world, to places no one had been to before.

She climbed mountains. She hacked her way through jungles. She even fought off a crocodile with the paddle of her canoe. And she did all of that wearing her olden-days dresses.

Then, when she finished travelling, she came back and built Ivy Lodge.

She stared down at me from her portrait, with her don't-mess-with-me eyes and a sniffy sort of look on her face.

I stared back. 'You built this house,' I said to her. 'What do you think of it now? All these new walls?'

I glared more. 'I know what *I* think,' I told her. 'I hate them...'

Just then I heard shrieks. Furious shrieks. Coming from above me.

I stopped glaring, and started chuckling. I knew who was shrieking, and why. And now I could hear feet thudding, a bedroom door bursting open—and here she came. Hurtling down the stairs, clutching her guitar...

Grace.

Grace is a teenager. Grown-ups are always saying to Mum and Dad that Grace is a Great Beauty.

I can't see it myself. I mean, she's got shiny black hair and a neatish nose. But she's also got a wide scowling mouth—especially when she looks at me. And her eyes may be big and grey, but she paints thick black lines all round them. Which make her look witchy and creepy.

'*Marbles*!' the Great Beauty was shrieking. 'Mum! Look! *Look!* MARBLES!'

Mum came running through the mum-door—just as Grace turned her guitar upside down.

I watched as marbles came tumbling out of the hole

in the middle of Grace's guitar, and went bouncing all over the lobby.

Then Grace turned on me. 'Is this because I am OK about the walls?' she hissed, right in my face. 'Not ecstatic—but *OK*? Is this because I said it was the best solution Mum and Dad could come up with? That if there is a wall between them, they can't actually yell at each other, like they used to? That us not having a big move, a change of school, is a good thing? That even split in HALF Ivy Lodge is actually bigger than lots of houses?'

I folded my arms. Sat there, staring and not speaking. Because I have seven ways of annoying Grace—but I find not speaking is the most effective.

Now Grace's teeth were grinding. 'Mum,' she said. 'He's doing the not-speaking thing. Make him stop. Make him speak.'

Mum just sighed. 'I don't think I can,' she said—and for some reason, she sounded weary.

Then Grace made a wailing sort of noise, and stomped off back up the attic stairs.

'Ned,' said Mum. 'Grace's guitar . . . That was unkind.'

I gaped at Mum. 'Was *unkind*? Was UNKIND?' I said, feeling so indignant I thought I might burst. 'No! What *is* unkind is you and Dad splitting up. And splitting Ivy Lodge in half. THAT is unkind.'

And I had more to say. 'When things are *my* fault,' I said, 'you make me say sorry and put things right. And now, this is YOUR fault. All the walls. And that's what you should do. Say sorry, both of you, and KNOCK THE WALLS DOWN. Put Ivy Lodge back how it was.'

Then I barged through the mum-door, and headed for the stairs.

**5**

The Junior playground of Craggelton Primary was full of kids when I got there. Kids shouting, kids yelling, kids running, kids lining up. All in early for the first day back.

I looked around for Bill. Where was he?

Then I spotted him—at the front of the line for our new class, Cutlass Class. Talking to our new teacher, Mr Franklin.

I stared. There was someone standing right next to Bill.

A girl...

A girl with corkscrew curls and big clompy boots. A girl who scowled, as soon as she caught sight of me.

Oh no. Oh NO. Not *her*.

I shot across the playground, fast as I could. I had to SAVE Bill from the girl. Get him away from her. Fast.

But just as I skidded over, Mr Franklin took something out of his pocket. Something blue, something shiny, something glinting in the sun.

I knew what it was straight away.

The *buddy badge*...

'I hear you were new last year, Bill,' Mr Franklin was saying. 'That makes you the best person to have the buddy badge.'

Then he handed the badge to Bill.

*Bill!* The buddy of that girl!

No. This could NOT be happening. How *unlucky* could I get?

I watched, shocked, as Bill beamed and clutched the buddy badge. 'Me!' he gasped, his eyes all round and shining. 'An actual buddy! *Myself!*'

He gazed down at the buddy badge like it was an Olympic medal. 'Mr Franklin,' he said, all earnest, 'I have a LOT of experience of being new in school. I know what it's like. Because I have been new THREE times.'

Then he pinned the buddy badge on and stood up very straight. 'I will not let my badge down,' he said, even more earnest. 'I will be Maddie's buddy all day long. All week. As long as she needs.'

I coughed. Loudly. Right beside him. Then— FINALLY—Bill turned and saw me.

He beamed at me. 'Ned,' he said, brandishing the buddy badge, pinned to his top. 'Look! Look! I am buddy—to Maddie! This is Maddie. Maddie Clodd!'

Then he beamed more.

And the girl—the Clodd girl—looked me up and down with those conker eyes. 'You again,' she said. Then she sniffed.

It got worse.

I took one step into our new classroom, and I felt my heart plummeting. Down and down—right into my socks.

Because the classroom had new tables. Circular tables. With seats built in. Not two seats like last year, but three.

*Three...*

A seat for me, a seat for Bill—and a seat for the new girl, the Clodd.

By dinnertime I'd had enough of Bill buddying the Clodd. Lending her his coloured pencils, explaining how things worked, and where things were. Hardly noticing me—his *best friend*—at all.

As for the Clodd, she had NO understanding of my friendship with Bill.

Because Mr Franklin got us designing costumes for BayDay—a special day in Craggelton, happening soon. And straight off, I told Bill my plan. 'Bill,' I said. 'We're going as an octopus. Four arms, four legs... we can build a *brilliant* octopus costume!'

I sat back, waiting for Bill to agree.

He didn't.

Because Bill was sitting there, with that dreamy look on his face again. 'I was thinking,' he said, 'I might go as a starfish. Because starfish are interesting and—'

'Bill,' I said, and I felt my head shaking from side to side. '*Bill!* We're being an octopus. I just told you.'

Then I noticed the Clodd. Sitting there, listening with—I had no idea why—her mouth right open.

'What?' I said.

The Clodd ignored me—totally. She looked at Bill. 'Does he always tell you what to think? What to do?' she said. 'And does he always butt in?'

Now, I could answer that. So I did.

'I am NOT butting in,' I told her. 'It's YOU who's butting in. I am *helping* Bill.'

But my extremely clear explanation didn't seem to be good enough for the Clodd. She raised one of her eyebrows and looked straight at Bill. 'Do *you* think he's helping?' she asked him.

Bill sat there, scratching his head. 'Er,' he said—and a shifty look crept across his face.

I stared. Why the shifty look? It was a simple question, with a simple answer. Yes, I *was* helping—that's all Bill needed to say. But he didn't.

And the Clodd stared at him more. 'You should do MORE thinking for yourself,' she told him. 'Exercise the thinking bit of your brain. That way it grows bigger. *Fact.*'

I glared at her. She stared back.

When the dinnerbell went, I grabbed Bill by the arm. That girl was trouble. I *knew* she was—and Bill had to be warned not to listen to her.

'OgI nogeoged togo togalk togo yogoogu ogalogonoge,' I said to him, speaking Oggish.

Oggish is our secret Tower Two language. Because there's a whole chapter in *Secret Sleuth* on creating secret languages. And Oggish—putting *og* before each vowel—is brilliant, the best one. Me and Bill often use Oggish. And I had been practising Oggish at least fifteen minutes a day all summer—which means I can speak it really fast.

Bill had clearly NOT been practising Oggish over the summer. He stood there, frowning. 'Er,' he said, staring at me, 'I got the 'I need' bit but—'

'He said, 'I need to talk to you alone,' said the Clodd.

Then she turned to me and shook her head. 'Beginner secret language. VERY basic,' she said, conker eyes staring at me. 'Besides, it's rude to use a secret language in front of someone new.'

\* \* \*

The whole day was annoying like that. Then, when the bell rang for home time, Mum and Isabel were waiting for me by the Junior gates—which was also annoying. Because I do NOT need walking to school, *or* home. I go on my own now.

I marched over, and saw Mum had a frown on her face. A worried sort of frown, not a cross one.

'Ned,' she said, as we walked up the road. 'I had a call from your teacher today. About the morning register. He told me what happened.'

Ah. The morning register...

Mr Franklin—a smiley sort of teacher, not the shouty sort who thinks kids are a nuisance—got the register out and looked all round the class. 'And now, Cutlass Class,' he said, 'I get the opportunity to put some names to faces.'

Then he started the register. 'Maisie Adams,' he said.

Maisie's hand shot up. 'Here, Mr Franklin,' she said, waving. 'I'm here.'

Mr Franklin smiled at her. 'Maisie,' he said. 'Thank you.'

Then he looked down at the register again. 'Ned Arkle-Smith,' he said.

I sat there, not moving. Silent.

Mr Franklin looked all round the classroom. 'Ned Arkle-Smith?' he said again, eyebrows raised.

Other kids started shuffling, and fidgeting and looking at me. Then Maisie's hand shot up again. 'He's Ned,' she said, pointing at me. 'The one chewing his pen.'

Then I spoke. 'I *am* Ned, Mr Franklin,' I said— nodding politely, so he knew I wasn't trying to be difficult. 'But not Ned Arkle-Smith. This week I am Ned *Arkle*. And next week I shall be Ned *Smith*.'

'You will?' said Mr Franklin, looking baffled.

'Because of the wall,' I explained. 'Mum-weeks I'm an Arkle. Dad-weeks, I'm a Smith. Two houses, two names. See?'

It took quite a bit of explaining, but Mr Franklin *did* see… in the end. And, just like I hoped he would, he must have called Mum and told her about it. So here she was, looking all frowny and bothered.

Which was *fair*. Because if *I* felt all frowny and bothered—then so should Mum.

Mum sighed. 'Ned,' she said. 'I know you're not happy about the walls but—'

'No,' I said, before she could say any more. 'I am NOT happy about the walls. For once you are actually *right*.'

Then I stuck my nose in the air. 'And as for the register, I think it was perfectly reasonable,' I said. 'If you can split Ivy Lodge in two—then *I* can split my surname in two.'

And I marched off, fast, away from Mum and Isabel. Feeling fed up. Because today had NOT been a good day at school. I just hoped tomorrow would be better.

**6**

On Tuesday morning we had to bring in something from our summer holidays for Show and Tell.

When Mr Franklin called my name, I stomped to the front of the class. 'This is how I spent MY summer holidays,' I said. Then I opened the small box I was carrying, turned it upside down—and a whole lot of small plastic bricks tumbled on to Mr Franklin's desk.

Mr Franklin's eyebrows shot up. He sat there, looking startled, about to speak.

I held my hand up. 'There's more,' I said.

I picked the bricks up and stuck them all together to make a small wall. Then I waved the wall at Mr Franklin, and at the whole of Cutlass Class. 'Waiting for walls to be built,' I said. 'That was my summer.'

Then I stomped back to my seat, clutching my wall.

I sat down, glaring. Thinking about my dream last night. Because I dreamt I had magic powers, and sent Ivy Lodge spinning round and round, faster and faster—anti-clockwise, turning back time. And when Ivy Lodge stopped spinning—it was how it was before all the walls. How it *should* be.

I woke thinking it was true.

But now—oh no—my eyes were going all blurry. So I glared down at my trainers, as Bill got up and headed for the front of the class.

'This is my Show and Tell,' Bill said, beaming. Then he held up a big picture, a photo.

I stared. There was Bill, in a harness, clambering up a big wall studded with pretend rocks.

'I did a bouldering course this summer,' Bill said. 'On the climbing wall in the old water tower.'

He beamed more. 'And that girl there,' he said pointing at the picture, 'that's Lekeisha.'

And now Lekeisha was waving her hand and jumping up and down in her seat. 'Mr Franklin! Mr Franklin!' she said. 'I've got the *same* Show and Tell! A picture of me bouldering—with Bill in it!'

So Mr Franklin got them to SHARE their Show and Tell, to talk about bouldering together.

I sat there, shocked, listening to the two of them— Bill and Lekeisha—telling us bouldering tips.

'You have to warm up first,' said Lekeisha. 'And you have to think carefully before each move.'

Bill was nodding. 'That's a good tip, Lekeisha,' he said. And another good tip is that you have to focus on your balancing. And stay relaxed.'

'And you have to watch other climbers,' Lekeisha interjected. 'Other better climbers. Watch how they do it.'

Bill nodded. 'And when you finish you should warm down,' he said.

Lekeisha nodded too. 'Oh, and another good tip—'

On and on and *on*.

I sat there, shocked. Bill had a new friend.

But... Bill didn't NEED a new friend. He had me. Me and Bill, we were the Tower Two. A team.

Feelings, horrible feelings were squirming about inside me. Feelings I couldn't quite identify. Panicky feelings.

I knew that—of *course*—Bill must have done things over the summer. And I didn't want him to have been lonely. But all the same...

Bill was MY friend.

'Thank you,' said Mr Franklin when Bill and Lekeisha—FINALLY—stopped talking. 'And will you both carry on bouldering now you've tried it out?'

'Oh, yes,' said Bill, nodding. 'Me and Lekeisha have already signed up. We're doing bouldering on Thursdays after school.'

\* \* \*

That evening I sat in my room, fretting about Bill. And I do NOT like fretting, so I did what I always do to stop myself fretting.

Some sorting.

And today's sorting, I decided, was my sock drawer.

I laid all my socks out on the bed. I put all the spotty pairs together. All the stripy ones together. All the plain ones together. Then I lined them all up, darkest to lightest in each group. Then—carefully—I put them all up back in the drawer, in neat straight rows.

Better. Much better. Something I could control.

I never used to sort things. The first time I did some sorting was straight after Mum and Dad told us about the walls. I didn't know what to do, so I came up to my room and put all my books in height order.

Now I can't help sorting things. I've never been so tidy.

But sorting out my sock drawer didn't work. I was STILL fretting about Bill—so I went downstairs.

I'd make a hot chocolate. A big frothy mug of hot chocolate. In my favourite mug—my lemur mug.

Lemurs are number one of my top twenty-five best animals. Especially ring-tailed lemurs, like the one on my mug. It's the big round eyes I like. And the long stripy tail. And the way the ring-tailed lemur always looks confused. Like it can't make up its mind if it's a cat, or a koala, or a dog, or a squirrel.

Dad got me my lemur mug, and I always *always* have hot chocolate in it. So I marched to the mug cupboard and opened it and started searching.

I heard Mum come up the cellar steps, then into the kitchen—holding some tins of food, and shaking her head. 'No sign of that key,' she said. 'Can't find it anywhere.'

I glared at her. Who cared about finding a stupid key to a stupid door in the cellar? Not me. I had something MUCH more important to find. My lemur mug.

I searched and searched.

First in the mug cupboard. Then the other cupboards. Then the shelves. But there was no sign of my lemur mug. So—where was it? Where could it be?

Then I realized where …

In the dad-side. Along with the hairy beanbag.


Enough! I marched out of the mum-side and into the lobby. Then I hammered on the dad-door.

Dad opened it. 'Ned,' he said, looking surprised.

I marched past, heading for Dad's kitchen. Then I stopped in the kitchen doorway.

Dad's kitchen was full of grown-ups. All sitting round

his table. Five of them. But… who were they? I didn't know them. Not Dad's film club. Not his running club.

And I could smell lasagne. Dad's lasagne.

So these grown-ups—they were here for dinner. Not just any dinner. Dad's lasagne. My favourite.

I backed away out of the kitchen. Into the hallway. Angry. First, Dad should be cooking lasagne for ME. Second, how could I look for my lemur mug with all those grown-ups in the way?

'Ned,' Dad said, out in his hallway—and now it was Dad's turn to look all frowny and worried. 'I know it's tricky, but it's best you don't just turn up. It's best you call me first.'

My insides went weird. 'But—this is my *home*,' I said. 'This is Ivy Lodge.'

'It's also mum-week,' said Dad.

I gaped at him. 'What, so in mum-week I have to pretend this side of Ivy Lodge doesn't *exist*?' I said.

'No,' said Dad. 'Of course not. Just call me. Let me know you want to come round.'

Now I started to feel indignant. 'Call you?' I said. 'Like making a dentist or doctor appointment? You're my DAD.'

I stood there, gulping. I felt tears stinging my eyes—which was ANNOYING. So I blinked them back.

Then I glared. 'I have come for my lemur mug,' I said, as calmly and coldly as I could manage. 'And also the hairy beanbag. Where I go—they go. Kindly fetch them.'

Then I stuck my nose in the air. And glared more.

Dad sighed. But he went and found them both.

'Ned,' he said, as he handed them over, 'it's early days. We haven't worked everything out yet, but—'

'No,' I said. 'You haven't.'

Then I tucked the hairy beanbag under my left arm, hooked my lemur mug over my right hand, and marched out of the dad-side and into the lobby.

I felt cross. Miserable. First Bill, now Dad, making new friends. This had to STOP.

7

Back in my room I was sitting at my desk, glaring down at the driveway, when I heard the *thud thud thud* of small feet pounding up the stairs and—oh no—straight towards my bedroom door.

The door flew open, and in burst Isabel. Dressed in her elf pyjamas. Snow-white pigtails swinging from side to side. Cheeks pink and glowing.

She thudded over to me, carrying a big book. She stood on tiptoe and shoved the book as near my face as she could manage.

'Look at my bedtime story I got from the library,' she ordered.

I *did* look. I took one look—and I felt my teeth grind. That cover, that book. I knew it so well…

*The Bayeux Bathmat.*

The book that TRICKED me. The story of a boy who whizzed back through history on a magic time-travelling bathmat—to a real battle in England, called the Battle of Hastings.

It looked like a fact book, with a big square fact box on every double page. True fact boxes about the battle. About weapons. About a famous tapestry embroidered after the battle...

And a fact box about the bathmat... The material it was made of, its colour, its size, the shop the bathmat came from. And also the *spell* the boy did to make his bathmat go magic.

It fooled me. Utterly fooled me. I was thrilled. Thinking that because all the other fact boxes were true—so was this one.

So I tried the spell on *my* bathmat.

I followed the spell exactly. Then sat there, on the bathroom floor, staring at the bathmat, waiting. Convinced it would work.

It didn't.

And as I sat there, as the minutes ticked by— something clicked in my brain.

Maybe there was a *reason* the bathmat was not becoming magic. And also a reason nothing magic had happened to me yet. A reason magic only seemed to happen to children in books...

Maybe there was NO SUCH THING as magic.

* * *

I remember how it felt. All the feelings. The misery—the *agony*—of realizing the truth about magic. And the rage—the *fury* I felt.

And now, here in my room, with Isabel waving *The Bayeux Bathmat* right in my face—all those feelings came back. All those hopes I'd had—all those dreams. About magic, and how it might happen to me ...

Gone.

And they joined all the feelings *already* swirling about in my head. The miserable, confused, furious feelings. About the walls, about Dad and his new friends, about Bill having a new friend, buddying the Clodd ...

All the feelings I was trying and trying NOT to think about.

It was too much—all those feelings, swirling around in my head. Much too much.

Something snapped inside me. I found myself snatching *The Bayeux Bathmat* off Isabel. Then marching over to the window, flinging it open, and hurling the book as far as I could.

It landed, face down, in a flowerbed.

'THAT is what I think of your bedtime story!' I snapped, right in Isabel's face.

Isabel stood there, astonished, gasping, eyes popping, mouth open. Then her face scrunched right up.

'You BAD boy,' she roared up at me. 'You get my book back! Now! This very INSTANT! I shall count to ONLY three!'

'*You* get it!' I snapped back. 'It's a rubbish book! All lies! *Lies!* Because there are no magic bathmats—and NO SUCH THING as magic!'

Isabel gasped. She turned purple with rage. She started jumping up and down, stamping her feet. 'There IS magic. THERE IS!' she bellowed, wagging a furious finger in my face. 'Because there are elves! And elves are *magic*!'

Now her fingers were fumbling in the pocket on her pyjama top. 'And there is an elf in our GARDEN!' she bellowed. 'I spied it yesterday!'

Then she pulled out a tiny sheet of pale green paper. Then she brandished it right up at me.

Dear Human,
Thank you for the petal soup. It was very tasty.
Love from Elf Ellazora

'See!' she roared. '*See?* Elf Ellazora writ me a NOTE! Today!'

'Elf Ellazora did NOT write that note,' I snapped. 'Grace did, or Mum. Because there is *no* Elf Ellazora!

Because there are no elves whatsoever in the WHOLE WIDE WORLD!'

Then I snatched the little green note off Isabel.

I snatched it...

And I ripped it up.

Ripped it into tiny TINY pieces. And watched them flutter to the floor.

I was ashamed of myself—the moment I did it I was utterly ashamed of myself. It was a SHOCKINGLY mean thing to do to a four-year-old.

But then I heard a voice. A snapping voice—coming from the doorway. 'You should be *ashamed* of yourself!' the voice snapped.

I turned. And there was Grace. Scowling and tutting and pursing up her lips, as she looked at the note, shredded into tiny green pieces on the floor.

Now—Grace telling me I should be ashamed of myself when I already WAS ashamed of myself, really got on my nerves.

So...

'YOU should be ashamed of *yourself*,' I snapped back. 'First for all the rubbish guitar playing. Second for having a boyfriend like gruesome George. And third—just for BREATHING.'

It wasn't much of a comeback, but it was the best I could do.

Now Isabel started gnashing her teeth and doing more finger-wagging in my direction. 'That was my *special* note!' she roared, still purple with rage. 'From an ACTUAL elf! And one day you will be very extremely SORRY!'

'Ooh, I'm scared,' I said. 'Now get out!'

Then I pushed Isabel out of my bedroom. And slammed the door shut.

8

That night I had MORE dreams about walls.

Dreams of Bill and Lekeisha, climbing and climbing. Of Mum and Dad, of Grace and Isabel, all laughing, running about in a maze of gigantic brick walls. And me, on a bathmat, swooping around them all. Calling and calling—but not one of them listening.

Even Snapper and the Clodd barged their way into my dreams. Both pointing at a long winding staircase. Telling me there were lemurs at the bottom.

Lemurs!

I swooped towards the staircase on my bathmat. Flew down and down and down in search of lemurs...

But while I was busy swooping down the dream stairs—I was also busy walking down the actual, real-life stairs...

*Sleepwalking.*

Sleepwalking is something I've done twice in the

last year, and I do NOT like it. I don't know I'm doing it at the time. I just wake up where I shouldn't be.

The first time Mum found me asleep in the bath— the empty bath. Dreaming I was the sole survivor of a shipwreck, alone in a raft on an ocean...

The second time Dad found me in the kitchen, buttering a bagel. Dreaming I was lost in a dark gloomy forest. Wandering, scared and hungry, then finding a house. No one in it—but a bagel and some butter in the abandoned kitchen...

Somehow, those other times, I managed to sleepwalk without bumping into anything. As if, even sleepwalking, my brain knew exactly where everything was.

But *not* this time.

This time, I went sleepwalking down the stairs. Sleepwalking forwards into the lobby, and...

CRACK!

I woke up lying on the ground. With a very sore head—and a lump that was growing and growing.

I knew straight off I'd been sleepwalking. That my sleepwalking self had expected a big landing to sleepwalk along—and NOT a small lobby. Not all the new walls.

I could hear noises from downstairs—the TV. Some kind of noisy game show, with the audience laughing and laughing.

I was NOT laughing. I was furious. And in pain. My head was throbbing. Really throbbing...

And the thing about the pain is—it made me want to *blame* someone. Someone... or something.

So I glared at the wall, the dad-wall—and then I started talking to it. 'It was you,' I said, glaring. 'See this lump on my head? You did that. YOU!'

Look—I'm just telling you what happened. I'm not saying it makes sense. Not now. But it did at the time. Maybe I was concussed. Maybe I wasn't. Who knows? But whatever I was, I started to give the wall a good kicking.

'You're in the way,' I told it. 'Go and be a wall somewhere else. NOT HERE.'

Then, when the wall didn't reply, I just got angrier. 'Not talking?' I said. 'NOT TALKING?' And I kicked at it—hard—with my feet.

I stood there, in the lobby. Full of anger. HATING the walls. Hating every single wall I could see.

Because I had just realized something.

That—all this time, ever since that day Mum and Dad first told us they were splitting up—I had *never* given up hope. Hope that Mum and Dad would change their minds. That one day they'd STOP being split up and get back together.

But now I knew.

This lobby, the walls, all the walls—they were PROOF.

Mum, Dad … They would never change their minds. Never knock down the walls. It was just *not* going to happen.

Not EVER.

So I started kicking the wall more.

'You're a stupid wall,' I said, kicking it harder and harder. 'An EVIL wall. You're wrong, wrong, WRONG. You should NOT be here.'

Now I started pummelling the wall with my fists. Pummelling hard as I could. Kicking harder with my feet. Kicking and kicking and kicking—I could NOT stop kicking.

I felt that, if a boy could reach boiling point like water does—then I'd just reached it.

'I hate you,' I told the wall. 'Hate you. *Hate* you. HATE you.'

My eyes felt burning hot now. So did the rest of me. I felt blazing. *Sizzling*. Like I was bubbling and boiling, and on fire. Then a feeling whooshed right through me. Like a gigantic surge of POWER. Of ENERGY …

And *that* is when it happened.

When my pummelling fists, my kicking foot, went *straight through* the wall. Straight through it—as if it JUST WASN'T THERE.

I gaped. I rubbed my eyes. Stared at the wall. My fists... My foot... How did they do that?

It was impossible.

IMPOSSIBLE.

But it had just happened.

And then, standing there, staring, a thought thrilled right through me...

If my fists can go straight through that wall, and so can my foot—then, maybe, so can the REST of me.

**9**

I *did* it. I DID it!

I stared hard at the wall. Focused…

Then stepped right through that solid brick wall—as if it didn't exist. As if it just wasn't there.

But it WAS there. It was still there, clear as clear.

I stood in the dad-side, dazed. Staring at the wall I had just walked through.

How did I do it? How was it *possible*?

It wasn't possible. It was NOT possible.

But I had done it…

Somehow.

So—was it *magic*? ACTUAL magic?

No.

It was science. Some kind of science. It had to be. But… what *kind* of science?

I remembered something I saw on TV. A scientist, talking about how—one day—scientists might be able to create invisible gateways. So humans could pass through solid things...

Well, it looked like that day was here. That I—Edward Harrison Arkle-Smith—had actually *done* it. Created an invisible gateway. The first invisible gateway EVER!

Which made me a scientific phenomenon. A scientific *genius*.

No, not a genius—a WALLBOGGLER...

Yes, that was how I did it. Must be.

By the power of my mind alone, by the sheer FORCE of my anger as I stood there, raging at the wall, kicking at the wall—I *boggled* that wall. Bewildered it. Confused it. Made it so utterly boggled it STOPPED being a wall and started being a gateway. An invisible gateway.

Yes, that was how it happened. DEFINITELY.

But...

Now I was a wallboggler, what to do *next*?

I stood there, thinking. I could hear Dad downstairs, by his front door. Chatting and laughing, saying goodbye to his friends. Then the front door slammed and Dad went into the kitchen, whistling a cheery tune.

I thought about Dad—stealing the hairy beanbag and the lemur mug. Standing there, telling me I shouldn't just turn up. And cooking lasagne for his new friends, and now, doing the cheery whistling...

And I realized. Being here, in the dad-side—this was an *opportunity*.

So I crept along the landing.

Dad had photos, a whole row of them. Framed photos, family photos—hung all along one wall.

I rehung them all—upside down.

Then I tiptoed into his bathroom, scooped up a few things, and headed to his bedroom. I hid his toothpaste under his pillow. I hid his hairbrush in the pocket of his dressing gown. And I tucked his soap into one of his slippers.

I tiptoed away, chuckling to myself. There. Let Dad try and work THAT out. He knows I don't have a dad-key—because Mum and Dad had a talk with me.

*No keys, Ned*, they said. *Not yet. Not to start with.*

I knew why Mum and Dad said that. Because they thought I would use the keys for EVIL PURPOSES.

They were right. I would.

And I did *try* to find keys to the dad-side. I searched as hard as I could—but Mum is way too good at hiding things from a kid. She's sneaky, thinks of all the hiding places a kid will check. Then hides things somewhere they won't.

Well—now I had no need of keys.

And Dad would be boggled. Utterly boggled. He'd

know it wasn't Mum, know it couldn't be me. Have no possible explanation for who moved those things.

Then I had a thought. A brilliant thought.

Maybe Dad *would* find an explanation...

The Craggelton Hauntings.

I chuckled at that thought. Yes! That's what Dad would think. It was the Craggelton Hauntings—an old local legend—all over again.

The Craggelton Hauntings were supposed to have happened back in the olden days. Hauntings by a poltergeist. A vicious sort of ghost. A mean, nasty spirit. One that targeted houses with kids in. Bickering, fighting kids. Unhappy kids.

And the first Craggelton Haunting was right HERE. Not in Ivy Lodge—but in Moraggon Manor, the house that was here before.

The Moraggons were rich and ruthless, rumoured to have made all their money from wrecking. They were a quarrelsome lot—a huge clan, all living in Moraggon Manor. Always falling out with one another. Always arguing. Always fighting.

And worst of all were the two kids, ten-year-old twins, Drummond and Morwenna Moraggon.

The twins argued day and night. They fought and scratched and kicked and screamed. Then, one night, as Drummond pulled at Morwenna's pigtails, and she clawed at his face—a picture flew off the wall, and smashed into the mirror, cracking it in two.

From then on, the Craggelton poltergeist tormented the Moraggon twins. And the meaner the twins were to each other—the meaner the poltergeist got.

It tugged at their ears, it pinched their arms. It scribbled messages on their walls. It moved things and hid things, it hurled things and broke things. And it made noises at night—knocking, scratching, banging noises.

In the end, Drummond and Morwenna got too scared to sleep in the dark, so they secretly lit candles. But one windy night, a candle set fire to Drummond's bedroom curtains...

That was it. Moraggon Manor was destroyed, burnt down to the ground, and the Moraggon clan fled Craggelton, never to return. But the poltergeist did NOT flee. It stayed on. Visited other houses in Craggelton, house after house. Ones with arguing, fighting kids. And it only moved on once the kids had come to GRISLY ENDS—like falling down a well or tumbling out of a tall tree—trying to escape its pinches and punches.

It's just a stupid old legend, of course. And one with a boring ending. Because when the poltergeist moved in with the Tippett family, the legend says all three

Tippett brothers made a pact. *No more* fighting. Which made the Craggelton poltergeist fed up, so it left—and that was the last anyone heard of it.

Even so, mums and dads *always* bring it up when their kids are fighting. *Careful*, they say. *You'll start up the Craggelton Hauntings again.*

I smiled to myself. Yes, that's what would happen! Dad would take one look at the things I'd done and think—*straight off*—that he and Mum had brought the Craggelton poltergeist back by making us kids so unhappy.

And if that made Dad worried or scared or guilty—well, good. It served him right.

Wallboggling back was easy. I stared at the wall, and—*WHOOSH!*—the power surged right through me. Then with one step, with two—I was through the dad-wall and back in the lobby.

I went up the stairs, then wallboggled into my bedroom. I could NOT stop chuckling. What a skill! What a brilliant *brilliant* thing!

I sat at my desk. Thrilled. This had POSSIBILITIES. So many possibilities!

Would the government want a wallboggling boy as a *spy*? Could I could enter a TV talent show with a wallboggling act and make my *fortune*?

Maybe… But first—I needed a list.

I make lists ALL the time. I've got a big notebook full of lists. I started making lists the day Mum and Dad told us about the walls. I gave that first list a heading…

**Ten Reasons Mum and Dad are the Worst Parents EVER**

Since then I've given all my lists headings…

**My Five Best Dinners**
**Seven Ways to Annoy a Teenager**
**Twelve Reasons Mum Should Get Me a Pet Goat**
**Thirty-Two Reasons Custard Should Be Banned**

I started chewing the pencil. So first—the heading…

**Questions About Wallboggling**

I left a gap at the beginning of my heading—which I always do, so I can fill in the number when I've written my list.

Then I made a start on the questions…

**1. Am I the first—and only—wallboggler in the world?**
**2. Can I boggle ALL walls in Ivy Lodge?**
**3. Can I boggle all walls OUTSIDE Ivy Lodge?**
**4. Could I get RICH wallboggling?**
**5. Will I ALWAYS be a wallboggler?**

I stopped. I realized there were some other questions I needed to ask…

**6. Could I get STUCK while wallboggling?**
**7. Would getting stuck HURT?**
**8. Could I call the fire brigade to get me UNSTUCK?**

I chewed my pencil and looked at my list. Was that all the questions I could think of?

No. There was one more…

**9. Who do I tell about wallboggling?**

Then I had a thought. Maybe there was an even *more* important question…

**10. Who do I NOT tell about wallboggling?**

I stared at my list of questions. Then I completed the heading…

**Ten Questions About Wallboggling**

Shivers of excitement ran through me. My best heading, my best list EVER.

I had no answers to my wallboggling questions, not yet. But I would. Oh yes, I *would*.

Because this, tonight—it was only the START.

**10**

I ran to school on Wednesday morning. Bill *had* to hear about my wallboggling—the biggest, the best secret the Tower Two EVER had! And he had to hear soon, or I might *burst*.

But when to tell him? Not before school—not enough time. A secret this brilliant could NOT be rushed.

Dinnertime. That's when I'd do it. Down in the summerhouse, at the far end of the playground.

Yes! I could picture it now. I'd sit Bill down on the summerhouse bench, and whisper him the story of last night—the night I learnt to wallboggle. Take him through it, moment by moment. Watch his mouth drop open. Watch his eyebrows knot as he wondered whether to believe me…

Then I'd *show* him.

I skidded into the playground—every bit of me, toes to forehead, fizzing with excitement. Where was Bill?

There he was…

Oh.

He was chatting to Lekeisha.

I got the feelings again. The horrible panicky feelings.

Now Bill was nodding his head, and beaming. Then Lekeisha went skipping off to join Maisie Adams.

So I charged over to Bill, and grabbed him by his sleeve. 'Bill,' I hissed in his ear. 'Emergency meeting! Tower Two, this dinnertime, in the summerhouse!'

Then I waited. Waited for Bill's eyes to light up, for the Bill-beam to spread across his face, for his head to nod—and for him to flick his ear. The secret sign that he agreed to the meeting.

Because Bill knows I only call emergency Tower Two meetings in school for big reasons. Things that can't wait.

I called the first one to tell him I had found the skeleton of a rabbit—a *complete* skeleton. And the second to tell him I got a *Super Sleuth* lie-detector kit from my auntie.

And this—this was even BETTER!

But Bill just stood there. Then a big furrow scrunched its way right across his forehead. 'What's the emergency, then?' he said.

I felt lurches inside. This was not how it was supposed to be. NOT how I planned.

'Something top secret,' I told him. 'Something BRILLIANT! Something for the Tower Two *only*!'

Now Bill started scratching his head. 'Hm,' he said.

I stood there shocked.

*Hm?* Why was Bill saying *hm*? What was there to say *hm* about?

'There's a problem,' Bill said now. 'Me and Lekeisha are going to the library at dinnertime. We need to look at some bouldering films before tomorrow. I just arranged it.'

'*Unarrange* it,' I said—well, sort of demanded. 'UNARRANGE it! This is way more important!'

But Bill just stood there, shaking his head. 'I don't think I *should* unarrange it,' he said, slowly and carefully, concentrating hard. 'And that is for two reasons.'

I stared, as Bill started ticking reasons off on his fingers.

'The first reason is that I promised Lekeisha,' Bill said, 'and I think a kid who makes a promise should keep it. And the second reason is that I actually *want* to look at bouldering films this dinnertime.'

Now Bill was nodding, looking pleased with his thinking. 'So—as I can't do both and I arranged with

Lekeisha first—I think it's *you* who should rearrange the Tower Two meeting. To tomorrow dinnertime. Because I've got stuff to do at home later.'

I slapped my head in frustration. I could NOT help it. Bill had *no idea* the secret I had to tell him.

'Bill,' I said—well, sort of shrieked. 'See? SEE! This is what happens when you do too much thinking. You think all WRONG!'

Straight away—even though I was *clearly* right to point that out to him—Bill got a huffy look on his face. Then he stuck his nose in the air.

'I think a true friend would encourage me in my thinking,' he said. 'And I also think Maddie is right. That I should do MORE thinking.'

Then the bell rang, and Bill marched off to line up.

I stood there, reeling with shock. Panicking.

What was *happening* to Bill? How could he POSSIBLY choose the library with Lekeisha over an emergency Tower Two meeting with me?

Bill didn't *need* to be friends with Lekeisha. He had *me*. Bill was muddled. SO muddled.

Yes. That was it. Bill was muddled—and I had to HELP unmuddle him. Help him realize that Lekeisha was *not* someone he should go bouldering with, or to the library with. Or even have as a friend AT ALL.

Just one problem—I didn't know how to do it. Not yet...

'Exciting news!' said Mr Franklin that morning. 'One of you has won this!'

And he pulled something out of his cupboard. A jar—a *huge* jar—of Swizzlers.

The class started buzzing. Who was the prizewinner? What was the prize for?

Then Mr Franklin told us.

It was Bill.

Because, this summer, Craggelton library ran a competition. A poetry competition. *Poetry*...

Bill won it. For his poem: 'Ice Creams on the Beach'.

I sat there, dazed. As Bill walked proudly to the front of the class, kids were clapping and cheering. Then Mr Franklin handed him a prizewinner's certificate and the jar of Swizzlers.

We're not actually allowed sweets in school, so Mr Franklin took the jar back, and put it in his desk drawer until home time.

Then he started saying stuff about Bill being a credit to the class and the school. Blah blah blah—I wasn't really listening.

No.

I was sitting there tingling from head to foot. I had a plan for that jar of Swizzlers, a brilliant plan. Because that jar of Swizzlers—it was an *opportunity*.

I tingled all through dinner, thinking about my brilliant plan. I tingled lining up in the dinner hall. I tingled getting my tray.

And I tingled listening to Bill chatting to Lekeisha. Chatting about bouldering. Chatting about them both showing the Clodd round the library before watching the bouldering films. Chatting on and on and *on*.

Yes.

I sat there, tingling. Because all that chatting Bill was doing—my brilliant plan was going to put a STOP to it. Help Bill remember who his true friend was.

Me. Ned Arkle-Smith. Who saved his ACTUAL life on Sunday.

So, as soon as dinner was over, as soon as Bill went off to the library with Lekeisha and the Clodd—I sneaked off. Back along the corridor to Cutlass Class.

Because the classrooms are locked at dinnertime—that's the rules in our school. When the classrooms are empty, the teachers lock the doors. Which means there is no way for a kid to get in…

Unless the kid is a WALLBOGGLER.

* * *

I faced the classroom wall, then checked all around. Carefully. *Very* carefully. No one was in sight. No one to spot a wallboggling boy ...

It was time.

I stared. Focused. Then took a step forward.

But ... ow, ow, OW.

I could NOT boggle through. My knee, my head— they both clunked against something hard. Something cold.

I pulled myself back, away from the wall, baffled. What was that clunk? What was happening? Why did my wallboggling not work?

Then I realized why.

Because there was something up against that bit of the classroom wall. Mr Franklin's filing cabinet. A big steel filing cabinet, full of teaching stuff.

And—I supposed—as I was a wallboggler, and not a furniture boggler, I could *not* get through it.

I ran further along the wall. Checking all around. Desperate in case someone came round the corner. Spotted me mid-wallboggle. And *foiled* my brilliant plan.

I tried again. I tested the wall first by putting my hands through. Because I did NOT want another of those clunks.

But ... ow, ow, OW.

I pulled my hands back—fast. Because this time the pain wasn't a clunk. This time the pain was sharp and jabbing, and just in one finger.

I stared down at my finger. It had teeth marks on it. Tiny teeth marks. And I realized. Those teeth marks— they were Dumbledore, the class hamster. I must have put my fingers straight into his cage.

Now I was really panicking.

Calm down, I told myself. And think. Think, think, *think*. What else is in the room? There must be a bit of wall I can get through. But where?

I pictured the classroom in my head. Imagined walking in through the door. Seeing all the desks, Mr Franklin's desk facing them.

And on this wall—to the left, the filing cabinet. To the right, the nature table and Dumbledore. Then the class noticeboard. And then—a *space*. A bit of wall with NOTHING on it.

But now I could hear footsteps. And voices. Two voices. Grown-up voices. Teachers' voices. Miss Barker definitely. And one other.

The footsteps grew louder. Nearer.

Quick! I had to do this *now*—before they came round the corner and spotted me.

I stared. Focused. And then, I was *through*.

I stood there, inside the empty classroom, tingling more. Because there, at the front of the class, was Mr Franklin's desk, and the drawer with Bill's jar of Swizzlers inside.

So I headed straight for it…

'Cutlass Class,' said Mr Franklin, that afternoon, with a very serious look on his face. 'Someone has *stolen* Bill's jar of Swizzlers.'

Astonished whispers buzzed round the room. And I sat there, doing my best to look astonished—even though I wasn't.

'I believe one of you must have hidden in the art cupboard just before dinnertime,' Mr Franklin said. 'Stolen the Swizzlers, then used the opportunity to rejoin the class in the confusion caused by the wasp. That is the only way it can have happened.'

Because the moment we got into afternoon class, a giant wasp started buzzing around the classroom, and kids started squealing and running and dodging as it whizzed about.

It wasn't a bad theory—just completely wrong.

Mr Franklin looked around. 'I would like someone to own up,' he said. Then he waited.

I sat there, trying not to chuckle, knowing that no one could possibly guess my secret skill. Or my brilliant plan.

Now Mr Franklin sighed. 'I am going to have to search your bags,' he said. Then he walked round the class, searching every kid's bag. Until he got to Lekeisha. And there, tucked in her bag—was a jar of Swizzlers...

A half-empty jar of Swizzlers.

Lekeisha gasped. So did the whole class. Including Bill.

I sat there, waiting for Bill to be shocked. Disgusted that Lekeisha was a *crook*. A Swizzler-stealer. And NOT a suitable bouldering companion.

But Bill's hand shot up and he leapt to his feet. 'It can't be Lekeisha, Mr Franklin,' he said indignantly, shaking his head from side to side. 'She was with me all dinnertime. In the library. She has an ALIBI!'

Oh. Oh *no*.

I realized straight away—my brilliant plan had a FATAL FLAW.

And now Maisie Adams put her hand up. 'Mr Franklin, Mr *Franklin*!' she said, gasping. 'Lekeisha must have been FRAMED! Because if Lekeisha *was* the thief, the last place she'd put the jar of Swizzlers would be in her bag! We should check everyone for alibis. See who wasn't in the playground. Find the *villain* who framed her!'

Mr Franklin *did* check for alibis.

We all had one. Every single kid in class, including me, had been in the dining room, or outside at dinnertime.

Of course, there were quite a few of us kids who went to the toilets. But clearly none of us could be Swizzler-stealers, as the classroom door was locked...

No. It *had* to be an inside job.

The whole of Cutlass Class was buzzing with ideas. Here was a mystery, an actual real-life *mystery*—here, in school!

Just how did the Swizzler jar get into Lekeisha's bag? And who had eaten half of them?

I sat there listening. Feeling a bit sick, a bit thirsty. My stomach was making strange noises, and I never wanted to see another Swizzler again. EVER.

I didn't mean to eat so many. In fact, I didn't mean to eat *any*—but I just couldn't help it. They looked so tempting. And once I had one ... well, I had more.

But now—I felt bad. Sick. And guilty. A horrible combination.

In the end, Cutlass Class came up with three theories:

- **Mr Franklin stole the Swizzlers—but he wasn't letting on.**
- **Some kid found a secret passageway into the classroom.**
- **The Craggelton poltergeist did it.**

The Craggelton poltergeist got the most votes.

There was quite a lot of arguing in the playground after school about what the Craggelton poltergeist did with the Swizzlers. Some kids thought the poltergeist ate them. But most kids thought the poltergeist hurled them out of the jar and over the playground wall.

Then, as the arguing got more heated, some kids started panicking.

'This might just be the *start*,' gasped Josh Blink. 'First stealing the Swizzlers then—who knows? It might do more things. Worse things! We might all come to GRISLY ENDS!'

'We have to STOP arguing!' said Maisie Adams. 'That's why it came to Cutlass Class. Because we *do* argue, Mr Franklin said we do! Yesterday, remember? He said if arguing was an Olympic sport, Cutlass Class would win gold.'

'Maisie's right,' said Devinder Sembhi, knees trembling. 'We have to be kind children, nice to everyone—even kids we don't WANT to be nice to! *All* the time! That's the ONLY way to get rid of it!'

And, panicking most of all was Lekeisha. 'The Craggelton poltergeist is EVIL,' she said, teeth clacking. 'And it's coming after me. ME! Why *me*?'

'I'll protect you,' said Bill, patting her arm. 'I will NOT leave your side. I will ESCORT you home. In case the Craggelton poltergeist follows you.'

Bill? Escorting Lekeisha *home*?

No! I stood there, fed up. And—I just couldn't help it—I gave Bill a big scowl as he walked past with Lekeisha.

Bill's mouth dropped open. His eyebrows shot up. He looked at me, astonished. Then he frowned. A small frown. One that looked horribly as if Bill was thinking. Again.

I felt my shoulders slump as I trudged off home. How *wrong* could a plan go?

Then, behind me, I heard a voice. 'I know it was you,' the voice said.

I turned. And there she was, right behind me. Conker eyes staring.

'The Swizzler-stealer...' she said. 'I *know* it was you.

There is not one other kid in class who would come up with an idiot plan like that. Just you.'

She stared more. 'Although...' she said, thoughtfully, 'I know you're an idiot—but I didn't think you were mean. Trying to frame a kid... Eating Bill's sweets...'

I scowled—first at the Clodd, then at the ground. Mainly because I knew she was right.

It seemed like a brilliant plan when I did it, but now it seemed—well... *less* brilliant. And the more guilty I felt, the bigger my scowl got.

But the Clodd hadn't finished. 'Only thing is...' she said, 'I know you did it—but I can't work out HOW.'

Then she raised an eyebrow. 'Care to tell me?' she said.

'I have NO IDEA what you are talking about,' I said. Then I marched off up the road. Because of all the kids in Cutlass Class, the Clodd was the last one I would EVER tell about wallboggling.

Back home, Isabel was in the kitchen. Standing at her easel, in her green plastic painting smock—hard at work.

Isabel does a LOT of painting. Big splodgy messes that she gives long titles. This was one of them.

'Look at my painting,' she said proudly. 'Its name is

"Pink Bunny Wakes the Singing Rainbow". And it is for Mummy.'

I did look. A big sheet of paper full of swirls and drips and splodges—mainly pink and silver and green.

Mum was sitting at the table, on her phone. 'Yes, two inflatable mega-slides,' she was saying, 'one meet-and-greet dolphin, and one mermaid grotto. Thank you.'

Then she clicked off her phone and put it on the table. 'Done,' she said happily. 'The very last orders for BayDay!'

Mum is chief organizer of BayDay and her phone's always buzzing. It buzzed again now...

She picked it up. 'Ben,' she said, looking a bit surprised.

Ben... Dad...

Mum sat there listening, looking more and more surprised.

'No...' she said. 'No. He definitely hasn't... Are you sure? Maybe you—'

She listened more. 'No way,' she said. 'I just told you. I hid it. VERY well.'

Now she started looking a bit annoyed. 'No. It certainly was NOT me.'

I left the room and headed for the stairs, trying to keep the smirk off my face. I could hear Mum still arguing with Dad. And I knew why. Dad had found all my little changes. My wallboggling changes.

Up in my room I got out my box of shells.

Wallboggling... Bill still knew NOTHING about my wallboggling. Thanks to Lekeisha.

No. I did NOT want to think about Lekeisha. Or Bill escorting her home. So I lined all my shells up along my window ledge, in shape, then size order.

Half an hour went by. Another half an hour. Then another...

It was no good. My wallboggling news could NOT wait. Not until tomorrow dinnertime, like Bill said. I had to tell him today.

He must be home by now. And—whatever stuff it was that he had to do at home—he could *stop* doing it. Because I was calling that emergency Tower Two meeting right NOW.

**12**

Swizzlers… I'd take a bag of Swizzlers to Bill's. To make up for his jar of Swizzlers being half-eaten by the Craggelton poltergeist.

I shot out of the Ivy Lodge front gates, and down the road into town. Then I hurried through the back streets, and on to the seafront.

I headed along the prom, which is a long one, full of shops: souvenir shops, gift shops, bucket and spade shops…

I made straight for Rita's, the best sweet shop in town.

It was a breezy sort of day, waves rippling and slapping themselves against the rocks out in the bay. Down on the beach, a plump dog was chasing a ball thrown by a plump lady. Two kite-flying kids were racing across the sand, kites soaring above them. And a mum was calling out, warning her kids to stay away from the cliffs because of loose rocks.

I bought the biggest pack of Swizzlers I could at Rita's, then hurried along the prom. This was it! Bill was FINALLY going to see my wallboggling.

I'd give him the Swizzlers and declare the emergency Tower Two meeting open. I'd tell him the first item on the agenda was the biggest secret we have ever had—then boggle out through his bedroom wall, and back in again.

Yes. That's what I'd do.

Then, when Bill recovered from the shock, we could start making plans. BIG plans. Planning wallboggling activities for the Tower Two every single day of the week.

And best of all, Bill would forget ALL about being friends with Lekeisha—because a wallboggling friend was *way* more important than a bouldering friend.

'Sorry Lekeisha,' he'd tell her tomorrow, with a sad shake of his head. 'But I can't do bouldering any more. In fact, I can't even be your friend any more. Because something much more important has come up. Something top secret and brilliant.'

Yes. That's what would happen. DEFINITELY.

And he'd drop the starfish idea too, be an octopus with me on BayDay—then things would be right again.

How things *should* be. How things *were*, before this summer got in the way.

It's about ten minutes along the prom from my end to Bill's. But I hadn't gone far when someone darted out of a side street...

Snapper.

He leapt straight into my path, then stood and stared. He snapped his fingers and pointed at the Swizzlers. 'I'll have them,' he said.

I held them closer and stared back. 'You will NOT,' I said.

Snapper came right up close. Stared harder at me—a shifty, twitchy sort of look on his face. 'I think you'll find I *will*,' he said.

Then he gave me a shove—a BIG shove. One that sent me staggering backwards and into a wall. He grabbed the Swizzlers out of my hand, and ran off.

I stood there, fed up. 'How did you turn into such an IDIOT?' I yelled, as Snapper disappeared along the prom.

There was no point running after him. Snapper could outrun me—he always could. Every time we raced on the beach he outran me.

Because me and Snapper were friends once. Not

from school—Snapper never went to Craggelton Primary. He went to the school his dad taught at. In Sheercliff, five miles away.

No. Me and Snapper met on the beach. I was four years old, and trying to snap my fingers. Snapper was five, and he taught me to do it.

He was always snapping his fingers—that's how he got his name. And he was always on the beach. Usually grubbing about in the rock pools. Because Snapper had big dreams back then. Unusual dreams for a five year old. Dreams of becoming a world-famous marine biologist, with his own TV show.

When Snapper was six, he got a big magnifying glass. He was VERY proud of it, took it everywhere. But one day me and Snapper were down in the rock pools when we both spotted a shell—a brilliant shell, all patterned and swirly.

We both made a grab for it, both got a hand on it. I said it was mine, he said it was his, then we had a big scuffle. And in that scuffle I stumbled right on to his magnifying glass...

It broke. *Shattered*.

Snapper RAGED at me, convinced I'd done it deliberately—which I hadn't. And that got me raging back at Snapper, so we had a BIG falling out.

We've never really spoken since—but after that, the pranking started.

But this... This was different. Shoving, stealing, bullying. I felt angry, frustrated. What was *up* with Snapper?

I walked on. On and on. I could see Bill's road, curving up in the distance, and a little kid on a scooter whizzing up to the last shop on the prom, the bait shop.

He propped his scooter up and went inside. And then, there was Snapper. *Again*. Scurrying out of a side street, towards the scooter.

He turned his head, quick turns, right and left. Then darted forward and gave the scooter a big kick. Knocked it right over, kicked it again and again right into the gutter.

I stood there, shocked. That was so *mean*. That poor little kid; his scooter was going to have big dents in it.

But then I spotted something that drove all thoughts of Snapper and scooters right out of my head.

Two kids from Cutlass Class, Harriet and Errol. Walking round the corner—and heading straight for Bill's road...

I stared.

Harriet and Errol, sauntering along... Were they going to see Bill? They could be. I *had* to find out.

So I shot into the next side street and ran up the back streets towards Bill's, fast as I could. Then, panting, I hurtled into the side alley by Bill's house, the perfect spot for some spying.

I poked my head round the wall—and here they came. Harriet and Errol, still sauntering, heading straight towards Bill's front gate.

But… why? What were they doing here? Bill wasn't their friend.

But then, I thought—he wasn't Lekeisha's friend either. Not until this summer…

And now Bill was opening his front door, beaming his Bill-beam as he let Harriet and Errol into his house.

Quick! *Quick!*

I checked all around. No one in sight. No one to see a wallboggler at work.

So I stared at the wall and—WHOOSH!—I stepped straight through the wall and into Bill's downstairs toilet, just like I knew I would.

I tiptoed out of the toilet and towards the stairs, I could hear voices in the kitchen. Bill, Harriet, Errol—all talking to Bill's mum about having some popcorn.

Then I heard feet, heading out of the kitchen.

I knew what that meant. Any second now those

feet would head for the stairs, and Bill's bedroom. So I shot up there first. Then wriggled my way under his bed.

Oh no.

Under the bed—the worst hiding place in the WHOLE room. It was dusty. It was uncomfortable. And there was a LOT of rubbish. Scrumpled bits of paper, old sweet wrappers, chewed pens, and bits of gum. And one big drawer on wheels taking up half the space, so I was squashed up one end.

Why oh *why* did I choose to hide here? Why didn't I hide in the wardrobe? That would have been way better. Roomier, and I could have pulled the door almost shut, but not quite. Left a tiny crack open, so I could see out, but they couldn't see in.

But now, here, under the bed—all I could see was FEET. Three pairs of trainers. Sparkly lilac ones—Harriet's. Very new, very clean ones—Errol's. And scuffed ones, with the laces undone—Bill's.

Then—*thud thud*—Harriet and Errol plonked themselves on Bill's bed. The mattress sagged down through the slats of the bed, and the heels of four trainers were close to my face.

'So,' said Harriet, 'the bouldering stuff... Can we see it?'

The bouldering stuff? Why did they want to see the bouldering stuff?

'It's all under my bed,' said Bill. And now I could see Bill's knees. He was kneeling down—just inches away from my nose.

No!

I panicked. What to do? I huddled, small as I could. *Please,* please *don't let him see me*, a voice said in my head, again and again.

And here came Bill's hands, grabbing at the ends of the drawer. He pulled it out and I relaxed. He hadn't spotted me.

Now I could hear Bill's hands rifling through the drawer. 'It's in here somewhere,' said Bill's voice. 'I'm sure it is.'

Then he paused. 'Or did I just shove it under the bed?'

Noooooo!

I shrunk as tiny as I could. But it was useless. If Bill looked under the bed—even one quick look—he'd see me huddled there. Listening in...

'Oh, here it is,' said Bill. 'Got it! Tips for beginners, contact details, everything.'

I slumped. Saved.

'Have you told Ned about us doing bouldering too?' said Harriet.

Bill sighed. A big heavy sigh. The sort of sigh a mum might give a tricky toddler—one having a meltdown about putting its socks on. NOT the sort of sigh Bill should do when thinking of me.

Then he spoke. 'Ned's already fed up about me bouldering with Lekeisha,' he said, doing the sigh again. 'He'll be even MORE fed up about you two.'

'He could be a boulderer too,' said Harriet. 'He's nimble—and he's got strong fingers. He does good knots.'

Errol gave a snort. 'Ned? Do bouldering?' he said.

Now Errol jumped up—and the mattress sagged a bit less. I could see Errol's gleaming white trainers stomping round the room. Then he put on a voice. A barking sort of voice.

'Bill,' he barked. '*Stop* the bouldering straight away. *I* decide what we do—and we do NOT do bouldering. And stop having any friends except me!'

I felt my jaw drop. Actually drop. The cheek of it! Errol doing an impression—a totally *wrong* one—of me. ME!

Then Harriet started tittering. 'Errol, that was mean,' she said. 'Mean... but accurate.'

It was so hard, staying crouched where I was. Listening.

I didn't *want* to crouch. I wanted to leap out and yell at them both. I was a good friend to Bill. I *was*. He liked the way our friendship worked.

And now Harriet started sighing, just like Bill did.

'Ned's always been bossy, always liked being in charge—even as a little kid,' she said. 'But he's got a LOT worse this year.'

Then Bill spoke. 'Ned...' he sighed. 'He sort of— *relies* on me. And he doesn't really have other friends. But I think—'

Bill stopped. His mum was calling. The popcorn was ready.

And straight off, three pairs of trainers thudded out of Bill's bedroom, along the landing and down the stairs.

13

I crawled out from under Bill's bed, reeling with shock. Then I tiptoed downstairs, boggled out through the toilet wall, and into the alleyway—just as a shape went whizzing past.

Snapper.

I shivered. A lucky escape. A few seconds earlier and he'd have spotted me wallboggling. And if Snapper discovered I had that sort of skill...

Well, I'd just have to make sure he NEVER did.

I marched off home—feeling indignant now.

Errol doing that impression... Harriet calling me bossy... And Bill... I could hear him now. That sigh, what he'd said. '*Ned—he sort of... relies on me.*'

How had Bill's thinking got SO muddled?

I did NOT rely on him. It's just that we were the Tower Two, a team—and that's the way it should stay.

And worse, he almost seemed to feel SORRY for me. Saying I had no other friends...

Bill was wrong.

Of *course* I had other friends, FAR more friends than Bill. How could I not have? I've lived in Craggelton my whole life. Bill has only been here one year.

Except, as I marched, I thought. My friends... they had ALL let me down.

Harriet, for a start. She was my friend in Infants, and I taught her lots of knots sailors use. But she is *not* my friend now. Not since the donkey.

It was a few years back, and we were being the donkey in our school Christmas play. I was the front end, and Harriet was the back. I showed Harriet my donkey walk, then she showed me hers.

My donkey walk was EASILY best—but did Harriet admit it? No. Then she said she was doing her walk, and I could do mine.

So I said no. That both ends of the donkey had to walk the same way, and we were walking *my* way.

But Harriet has a VERY stubborn streak. So, instead of her agreeing I was right, we had a big row. And now we hardly ever speak.

And Errol, the same. Because me and Errol fell out too, about three years ago. Errol's fault ENTIRELY.

We were building a sand monster on the beach. I said it should have spiky wings and a spiky mane.

Errol said it should have curly horns and a long curly tail.

I said no. Curly shapes were not monster shapes, spiky shapes were.

But did Errol listen? He did *not*—because Errol has a stubborn streak just as bad as Harriet's. He said maybe the monster could have spiky wings and warts *and* a curly tail and horns.

So I said no. We were doing a spiky monster, and that was that.

And then—for *no good reason*—Errol threw down his spade and marched off, muttering and scowling.

And Jacob, Maisie, Josh, Ella, Ollie...

They ALL had stubborn streaks. And because of those stubborn streaks, not one of them was still my friend. Just Bill.

But, as I walked—a thing happened that I was NOT expecting. A niggle started up in my brain. A tiny niggle. An annoying, questioning sort of niggle. *Are you sure it's them who have the stubborn streak?* the niggle went. *Are you sure?*

Well, I had NO IDEA what that niggle was doing in my head. It had no *business* being there, asking stupid questions. So I CRUSHED that niggle down, hard as I could.

Because, yes—it clearly WAS them.

And Bill was all muddled. Because somehow, over the summer—with the bouldering—Bill had forgotten who his actual TRUE friend was.

Me.

So I had to find a new way to help Bill. To remind him *I* was the friend he needed. Not all the others.

But how? *How?*

Then, just like that—a plan popped into my head…

I'd find a NEW friend.

Yes! That was the way to help Bill.

Bill would see me, laughing and joking with my new friend, and then Bill would get the horrible panicky feelings—just like I was getting. And he'd understand. He'd start thinking the way he *should* be thinking. Then—FINALLY—I could show Bill the wallboggling.

Yes. This plan was one of my best. A plan that would most definitely work. I just needed to find a kid to be that new friend.

But who? Who could I make my new friend?

I turned off the path, and walked up the road towards Ivy Lodge, thinking hard. Then I saw her, mooching about in the front garden of Vine Cottage…

The Clodd.

\* \* \*

It was tricky—but I had to do it. My future with Bill depended on it.

So I grinned at the Clodd. A real stretcher of a grin. Right across my face, ear to ear. The sort of grin a boy who was REALLY pleased to see someone would grin.

Then I waited for the Clodd to grin back.

She didn't. She stared. Then she narrowed her eyes. 'What's with all the grinning?' she said.

Oh. This might be trickier than I thought.

'I just thought…' I said, 'we could be friends. As we're neighbours.'

She stared more. Narrowed her eyes more. 'You're up to something,' she said. 'I know you are. And why would I want to be friends with a power-crazed idiot? A control freak like you?'

I tried not to grind my teeth—but it was hard.

Now the Clodd was leaning closer. She stared right at me. 'You've got pig eyes,' she said. 'Red as red. You've been crying.'

It's a side effect of wallboggling, red eyes. All that staring and focusing. 'I have NOT been crying,' I said.

The Clodd stared more. 'Whatever,' she said. Then she got out a bag of Swizzlers.

She held out the bag. 'Want one?' she said.

I did NOT want to eat another Swizzler, ever. But, just in time, I remembered my plan.

'Thank you,' I said, taking a Swizzler and stretching the grin out once more.

The Clodd was chewing hard. Doing more of the staring. 'You don't want to be my friend,' she said, thoughtfully. 'I *know* you don't. So this is some kind of plan.'

She stared closer. 'But what's the plan about?' she said. 'Something to do with Bill? Him having a chance this summer to realize how much of an idiot you are? And Lekeisha having a chance to realize what a nice kid he is?'

She paused. 'And maybe not just Lekeisha. Maybe other kids too,' she said.

She started nodding. 'That's it,' she said. 'He's made *more* friends. That's what you've just found out.'

My teeth starting grinding before I could stop them. This was NOT how the Clodd was supposed to behave.

Then the Clodd started nodding more, as well as chewing. 'I get it,' she said. 'You think that if Bill sees you with an ACTUAL friend of your own, he'll get jealous of you having a friend—just the way you're jealous of him having other friends.'

Jealous? Me?

'I am NOT jealous,' I said.

And I wasn't. I just didn't like getting the horrible panicky feelings all the time. It gave me stomach ache.

'Looks like you are to me,' the Clodd said. 'And it won't work. Only way you can be Bill's friend is by stopping being such an idiot yourself.'

I stood there, glaring at her. Just as a voice—high-pitched and piercing—rang out.

'Maddie!' the voice bellowed from the side of the garden. 'Where *are* you? I am ready to make the elf house!'

**14**

The Clodd and Isabel were friends—I had no idea how, or when, but they were. And they had plans to build an elf house. For the elf living in our garden...

Because Isabel came hurtling over to the wall, eyes shining, and looked up at the Clodd. 'I saw her, Maddie! Elf Ellazora!' she said. 'AGAIN! By the shed! She was small as my hand.'

The Clodd was nodding. 'She's definitely a garden elf, then,' she said. 'All garden elves are small. Except the Russian ones. They're a lot bigger. About this size.'

I gaped, as the Clodd held out her hands to show Isabel the size of a Russian elf. Then, before I knew it, the Clodd had hopped over the wall and into our garden.

She turned to me. 'So... you helping?' she said.

And Isabel started jumping up and down. 'Yes, Ned, yes! Help me and Maddie make the elf house!' she said. 'Help us make it!'

I gaped, first at the Clodd, then at Isabel. 'Me?' I said. 'Me! Why would I help make an *elf house*?'

'What else are you going to do?' the Clodd said. 'Sit in your bedroom, plotting ways to force Bill to be your friend? Sorting all your books into alphabetical order?'

I spluttered and—once again—my teeth started grinding. That was *exactly* what I was planning to do.

Then she stared at me. 'And you know what,' she said. 'You should be nicer to Isabel. Sisters are a good thing to have. A very good thing.'

And, if I'd been in a noticing sort of mood—I daresay I'd have noticed the Clodd's face went all sad. But I wasn't, so I didn't.

Instead, I gave up TOTALLY on the idea of making the Clodd my friend. And marched off to the front door.


I let myself into the lobby, and there was Dad—carrying lots of shopping and putting his key into the dad-door.

I glared. 'It's still mum-week,' I said. 'So what am I supposed to do? Ignore you?'

'Of course not,' Dad said.

'So ... we can speak?' I said.

'Yes, Ned, we can speak,' Dad said, with a small sigh.

'For how long?' I said. 'Is there a time limit? Are there set topics? The weather? My homework?'

'Ned—' Dad said. But I didn't wait for an answer. I just pushed the mum-door open, went through it and slammed it—HARD—behind me. Then marched off towards the kitchen.

And there was Mum.

She must have heard the slam. She turned. Took one look at me, and she did the small sigh, just like Dad did.

Mum... Dad... Bill... Why was EVERYONE sighing today?

Then Mum spoke. 'I know you're finding this hard, Ned,' she said. 'All the walls... the changes... everything.'

Well, Mum was right for once. 'Yes,' I said. 'I AM finding it hard. And I have a few questions.'

Then I jabbed my hand at the kitchen calendar. 'Sports day is in mum-week,' I said. 'I checked. But it's *Dad* who does sports day. So does Dad come to sports day, or not? And my birthday is in mum-week—so what happens then? Does Dad come round on my birthday, even though it's mum-week? Or does he have to sing me "Happy Birthday" through the KEYHOLE? And leave my present in the LOBBY?'

'Ned—' said Mum. 'Of course he'll see you on your birthday. And, yes, he'll do sports day.'

But I carried on. I felt furious. Fed up and muddled.

Because seeing Dad in the lobby for a few snatched seconds—it was worse than not seeing him at all. And it made me ache. Made me sad. And I do NOT like feeling sad. So I made myself feel cross instead.

'And disease...' I said. 'Suppose I develop a horrible disease in a mum-week? Suppose I am struck down by bubonic plague? Suppose I only have *hours* to live? Will I have to speak my dying words to Dad by phone? Or, suppose a man-eating *tiger* escapes from the zoo and gets into the mum-side? Do we have to call and check it is *convenient* to take shelter in the dad-side? How is this GOING TO WORK?'

Back in my room, I slumped at my desk.

What was the POINT of being a wallboggler? I hadn't done anything interesting. And instead of Bill being astonished, Bill didn't even know. *No one* knew.

There MUST be something better I could do with this skill. Something brilliant. But what?

All I could think of to do were bad things. Things that were wrong.

Like sneaking into Craggelton cinema without paying. Or cheating in tests by popping through the staffroom wall to check the answers. Or raiding a music shop at night, and helping myself to a drum kit.

No. I couldn't do those things. I didn't want to. So what *could* I do?

If this was the movies I'd do something better. Something brilliant. Something THRILLING.

I'd be a spy. A government spy. The Prime Minister would hear about my wallboggling and summon me to a meeting. Then send me on missions all over the world. And the missions would be full of danger, and daring, and astonishing gadgets.

Yes, that's what would happen in the movies.

Or I'd be a superhero—Wallboggling Boy. I'd have a cape with a big WB on it. And I'd discover a secret society—evil villains dressed in weird costumes—plotting fiendish plans in a secret room deep underground. Only one thing standing between them and success.

Me.

I stopped.

A secret room…

We didn't have a secret room here in Ivy Lodge—not as far as I knew. Not a *secret* room. But we did have a LOCKED room. A locked room inside the cellar, the door with the missing key. The one with no way in…

I stood by the entrance to the cellar and checked all around. No sign of Mum, or Grace, or Isabel.

Good.

This was MY secret. No one else's.

I opened the cellar door, quiet as I could. Then scuttled down the wide stone steps.

It's big, the Ivy Lodge cellar. It stretches right under the house. I stood there, in the middle of the flagstones, five wooden doors around me.

Four doors, all open. All full of stuff. Tins of food. Cans of paint. Broken things. And in one, a big boiler, humming and thrumming.

Just one door—shut. Shut and locked, but with no key.

The Arkle archive, that's what Mum calls the locked room. She says the Arkle archive is full of precious things. Documents, letters, photos, all sorts. The history of the Arkle family. Things she's going to sort one day, when she has time. Things she doesn't want messed with.

That's why she locked the door.

She has done ever since she found me down here as a four-year-old, scribbling with crayons on Grandad's birth certificate.

But a few years ago, Mum was putting a box of old photos in there, and she dropped the key after she locked it up. The key went bouncing off across the flagstones—and there are so many holes and dips and dark corners, and bits of old junk piled up against the walls, that Mum hasn't found it yet.

So no one has been in the locked room since then…
Until now.

It's a long time since I was there in that room, scribbling on Grandad's birth certificate. My memories were of it being dark and dusty, with no windows. And I remember standing on tiptoe to reach the light switch.

So I boggled my way in—and felt along the wall.

There it was.

I pressed the switch down, and a bulb glowed dimly from the ceiling.

I looked around.

It was cobwebby in here. Cobwebs on everything. And dusty, with things lurking under dusty sheets, and stacked up in dusty boxes.

BUT…

As a secret den—MY secret den—it had possibilities.

I just had to clean it up. A lot.

I jumped. A *huge* spider, black and hairy, scuttled across the floor. Then out under the door.

Well, I didn't mind that. I like spiders, especially hairy ones. I'd be happy to share my den with a few spiders.

But the dust—that would have to go. It was tickling my nose and making my eyes itch.

Then I sneezed. Once, twice, three times. And big clouds of dust shot up in the air, from a dusty sheet straight ahead, draped over a big bulging shape.

I went over. Whatever was under there might make a good table for my new den. So I pulled the sheet off.

There was a big chest underneath it. No, I realized... Not a chest, a *trunk*. A huge trunk, like a giant's suitcase. The sort of trunk olden-days people—rich people— used as luggage when they went travelling.

The trunk had big brass hinges, and paper labels stuck all over it. Olden-days labels, with interesting names on them...

**Cunard Shipping Line**
**Roma Hotel**
**Venezuela**

And it also had two big initials in gold...

**𝔐 𝔄**

M A... Matilda Arkle, the woman in the portrait, the olden-days relative . . .

It was her trunk—it must be.

I clicked the big brass hinges, and lifted the lid.

The trunk was split into two halves. One half had a jumble of stuff—childhood things. Olden-days toys. A battered wooden duck on wheels. A skipping rope with painted handles. A doll's house. And a creepy doll with a waxy face and shiny blue eyes.

The other half was full of books. Lots of books. And, right at the top—a big leather book. Dark blue, with a padlock, and a key on a chain.

I turned the key in the padlock, clicked it open, then turned to the inside front page.

DIARY, it said, in gold lettering.

Except whoever it belonged to had crossed out diary—with a VERY firm stroke of a pen—and given it a new name.

## MY BOOK OF SECRETS

*Begun, this First Day of January,*
*By Matilda Emmeline Arkle,*
*Aged Almost Ten Years.*

I turned the page. And there was the first of January.

This book calls itself a diary—but I say PAH! to that. A diary is for DULL girls. Ones who wish to record the events of each day. Meals that were taken, lessons that were studied, outings enjoyed.

I shall NOT do this.

I shall share my SECRETS. I shall tell this book how I feel. And of all the WRONGS that are done—again and again—to me.

By my father, who laughs and pats me on the head when I tell him of my wish for a train set.

By my mother, who gasps, and says, 'no, no, no—a dolls' house is a FAR MORE suitable toy for a girl.'

A dolls' house! What, pray, would I—future fearless explorer of all corners of this globe—want with a DOLLS' HOUSE?

And most of all, the wrongs done to me by my GOVERNESS, the most horrible of creatures—with hair on her lip, a scowl in her eyes, and the smell of dead pike all around her.

So, dear Secrets Book, I shall begin the year with a list...

## Four Reasons I DETEST My Governess

1. She does smell of vileness — see above.
2. She is dull, yet cruel, a most unpleasing combination.
3. She cackles like a witch when I prick my finger on my needle.
4. She whispers tales of the child-catching bogeyman lurking in wait beyond the schoolroom windows.

That was it for the first of January. And I liked the sound of Matilda Arkle, so I turned the page.

On the second of January, Matilda was fed up with the clothes she had to wear. All frills and flounces, and loathsome petticoats, when what she wanted was the freedom of pantaloons—which I think was what boys wore.

She also wrote another list: Eighteen Ways to Destroy a Bonnet.

On the third, it was Matilda's tenth birthday...

She got the dolls' house. Then she wrote her next list:

## Five Fine Birthday Gifts for a Fearless Explorer

1. One pair strong boots — to withstand bites and swamp water.

2. *Canvas gaiters — to protect against leeches.*
3. *Hat, storm-proof.*
4. *Compass.*
5. *Revolver — in case of pirates.*

On the fourth, Matilda *did* write about the events of her day…

*My secret wish was — I thought — to be fulfilled today.*

*For, to date, I have been ALONE in my schoolroom. Seated in that airless room, day after day. Just me and my governess — teaching me things I have NO interest in learning. Such as sewing and singing.*

*And how I have LONGED for another child to share my schoolroom.*

*Today, that was to happen. Another girl was to join me. Lavinia Montmorency from the gabled house on the far hill.*

*How happy I was as I waited to greet Lavinia. How thrilled to have a companion of my own.*

*Until the moment I met her…*

I read on. Matilda and Lavinia were sent to the playroom that first morning, so they could make friends.

They didn't.

Lavinia is *impossible*. 'Play with the dolls' house,' I told her, 'while I ride the rocking horse.'

Did she do as I said? She did NOT. Instead, she whined, right in my face.

'I want to ride the rocking horse,' she whined. 'And I am the GUEST.'

I folded my arms and gave her the sternest of looks. 'I do believe it is MY rocking horse,' I said. 'And MY house. You will have to wait your turn.'

She pouted in a most unpleasant way. 'But I don't want to wait my turn,' she whined. 'And a girl with good manners would LET me ride the rocking horse first.'

I had heard enough. So I pulled her pigtails, as hard as I could—and off she ran, sobbing, to tell tales to my governess.

It was so UNFAIR. Because of that whining girl, Matilda's governess gave her something called lines.

Lines! What a *stupid* thing lines were. Writing the same boring sentence over and over again. This one:

A well-mannered young lady should NEVER pull another's pigtails.

By the end of the week Matilda was deadly enemies with Lavinia. And I wasn't surprised—having to put up with that girl, moaning all day long, refusing to do what Matilda said. No wonder she wrote one final list...

### Four Reasons Lavinia Is Woefully Wrong

1. She calls me Miss Bossy-Boots.
2. She has a very STUBBORN STREAK.
3. She does NOT admit that my ideas are better than hers.
4. She gives sharp pinches then pretends she has NOT.

I closed Matilda Arkle's Book of Secrets, for now. But I knew I would come back to read more. Definitely.

Then I boggled my way out through the wall—and straight off, I started thinking about Bill.

Tomorrow. Tomorrow was the day. It *had* to be.

Yes, tomorrow Bill would see my wallboggling. And nothing would stop that happening. Nothing AT ALL.

16

Thursday morning—and there was the Clodd. Waiting, as I came out of the Ivy Lodge front door.

She hopped over the wall as soon as she saw me.

I gave her a scowl, for *ruining* my plan to show Bill I had a new friend—then set off for school.

She set off beside me.

'So, the Swizzlers...' she said, staring at me with a gleam in her eyes. 'I thought about it ALL night. And there is only one way I can think you did it.'

She put her head on one side. '*Magic*,' she said.

I stopped, there and then. Did my best disbelieving snort. An excellent snort, a convincing snort. A snort I was proud of.

'*Magic?*' I said. 'MAGIC? *How* old are you? You're not some little kid. You're WAY too old to actually believe magic exists.'

Then I marched on. Calm on the outside, fretting on the inside. Why oh *why* would the Clodd not leave me alone? It was Bill I wanted to tell about wallboggling. NOT her.

But she clomped along, shaking her head. 'Can't prove a thing *doesn't* exist,' she said. 'Just that it does.'

I did the snort one more time, but she took no notice.

'Besides,' she said, 'magic's just a word. Maybe magic is actually *science*—but science humans haven't worked out yet.'

Then she tilted her head up. 'See that,' she said, pointing at a plane, flying high, a faint white trail spreading out behind it. 'If I was an olden-days cavegirl and I saw that flying through the sky, I'd call that magic. But we call it a plane.'

Now, I had to stop her there.

'If you were an olden-days cavegirl,' I said, 'first, you wouldn't ever SEE a plane and, second, you wouldn't call it magic. You'd just GRUNT. That's what cavegirls did.'

The Clodd shook her head. 'Wrong,' she said. 'There's experts who think cavegirls *did* speak. It's in *Fascinating Facts for Curious Kids*, volume one.'

I did NOT want to carry on this conversation, but I couldn't help it. The Clodd had to be put right.

'Well, if cavegirls did speak,' I said, 'they wouldn't say things like "Ooh, look, magic." They'd say things like, "Oh no, not mammoth for dinner *again*." Or, "Does this furry top come in any other colours?"'

'Whatever,' said the Clodd. Then she stared more.

'So…' she said thoughtfully. 'The pretend-snorting— it's clearly a cover-up. I know it is. You CAN do magic. But what sort? What do you do?'

She narrowed her eyes. Sucked in her cheeks. 'Is it teleporting?' she said. 'Is that what you do? Magic yourself from one spot to another?'

'I can NOT teleport,' I said. 'Now leave me alone.'

The Clodd didn't.

'So—if it's not teleporting…' she said thoughtfully, 'Is it slithering, then? Is that what you do?'

I gaped. 'Slithering?' I said.

'The classroom windows,' she said, thinking hard. 'They have locks on them. They only open a little bit. So a kid couldn't get through—*unless* the kid could flatten itself and SLITHER in…'

My jaw was starting to ache with all the gaping I was doing. Was the Clodd NEVER giving up?

It didn't look like it.

'So… how did you get it, then?' she said now. 'The slithering? Did you do a good deed for an old lady—a wish-granter in disguise? Did you find a lamp in a car boot sale, rub it, and have a genie whoosh out?'

She stared again. 'And why slithering?' she said. 'Why choose that? Of all the wishes you could wish? If I got a wish granted I'd choose flying. But choosing slithering—that's just *weird*.'

She stopped. 'Oh,' she said. 'Was it a cockroach? Did you get bitten by a cockroach?'

I felt my eyebrows knotting. A cockroach? What was the Clodd talking about?

'They can flatten themselves, cockroaches,' she said, still doing the thinking aloud. 'Make themselves thin as a piece of paper. So—is that it? Did you get bitten by a cockroach, and get cockroach powers? Slithering powers?'

I gaped.

'Shame it's you who got the slithering,' she said. 'Slithering's wasted on you. You're not the sort of kid who'll use it wisely.'

Then she stared. 'So... show me your slithering,' she said.

'I am NOT a slitherer,' I snapped. 'Now go away.'

At the gates, the first person I saw was Lekeisha. So I scowled at her, I just couldn't help it. Then I saw Errol and Harriet. I scowled at them too.

Clodd spotted the scowls, and straight off her eyebrows shot up.

'Know who you're like?' she said. 'Canute. That crazy king. The one who thought he could control the tide.'

I gaped at her. Canute? Why *Canute*? What was she talking about now?

Now the Clodd started nodding, looking wise—which she wasn't.

'You think you can control Bill,' she said. 'Who he's friends with. But you can't. Any more than Canute could control the tide when he tried—'

Well, I had to stop her there.

'Wrong,' I snapped. 'You are WRONG about Canute. The real Canute *knew* he couldn't control the tide. It's just he was sick of his courtiers telling him how powerful he was—so he showed them he wasn't. Stuck his throne on the beach, ordered the tide to stop coming in, then got soaked when the tide took no notice. And that shut them all up.'

I read that on page eighty-seven of *Fascinating Facts for Curious Kids*, volume two. How somewhere along the line the Canute story got twisted.

But telling the Clodd that made no difference. 'Well, be like the real Canute then,' she said. 'KNOW that you can't control Bill ... can't stop things changing.'

She was shaking her head now. 'You've got no power

over changes,' she said. 'The only power you have is how you deal with them.'

'When I want your opinion I will let you know,' I snapped. 'But I WON'T want it. Ever. About anything.'

I looked around. Where oh *where* was Bill? We had a meeting this dinnertime. At LAST. A meeting that was going to *change* things.

But there was no sign of Bill that day. Because Bill had the bug, the one going round the school, the one that four kids in Cutlass Class had today—which meant I was STUCK with the Clodd.

She spent a lot of the morning staring at me, looking as if she was thinking hard. Then, in the dinner queue— she started up with the questions. *Again.*

'So...' she said. 'If it's not teleporting and it's not slithering, what *is* it you do?'

I felt my shoulders slump.

'Will you give it a rest?' I said. Then I shuffled on, edging nearer the front of the queue.

The Clodd shuffled beside me. 'But however you do it,' she said, 'why keep it a *secret*? If I got a magic skill, I'd be telling every single one of my friends. I'd—'

She stopped. 'Oh,' she said. 'You haven't got any friends. Due to being an idiot.'

I glared at her. Then I took my tray from a dinner lady and marched off.

Our dinner trays have two bowls. One for main, one for pudding, both with lids. I sat down and opened my first bowl.

'Spicy chicken and noodles,' said the Clodd, sitting down next to me. 'Yum.'

I said nothing. Just ate as fast as I could.

Then I opened the pudding lid...

I stared down at my pudding. I stared and stared.

Then I started to quake. Because there, right there—spilling all over the top of a slice of apple pie—was the worst thing in the *whole* world. The thing I have nightmares about. Nightmares that wake me screaming in terror...

CUSTARD.

**17**

It was a shock. A horrible shock. This had NEVER happened to me before. *All* the dinner ladies know not to give me custard. All the dinner ladies, except the new one that had just served me...

Because there it was. Custard—thick and gloopy, and pale eggy yellow, dribbling all over the pie...

I felt my teeth clacking in terror. My knees wobbling. *Everything* wobbling.

I clutched at the Clodd's arm. 'Get rid of it,' I said. 'Get RID of it.'

A feeling was surging through me. A panicky, choking feeling. And I knew, I *had* to get away. Away from that terrifying bowl of slimy yellow custard.

So I leapt to my feet, kicked my chair back—and hurtled out of the dinner hall.

I charged outside and across the playground, gasping for air, trying to think about anything—ANYTHING—that wasn't custard. That big wobbling pile of custard.

But the more I tried *not* to think about custard, the more I *did* think about custard...

So I charged down to the summerhouse.

It's a quiet spot, the summerhouse. At the far end of the playground. A place where kids go to sit and think.

I sat in there, huddled on the bench, taking big deep breaths and—slowly, slowly—I felt myself calming down.

Then I heard feet. And there was the Clodd, standing in the doorway.

Why was she here? I did NOT want her here. So I stared down at a big knot in the summerhouse bench. 'Go on, then,' I said, feeling grumpy. 'Laugh. That's why you're here, I know it is.'

The Clodd didn't laugh. She just rolled her eyes. 'How can one kid know SO little about SO much?' she said, which made me feel even grumpier.

Then she sat down. 'It's got a name, fear of custard,' she said. 'An actual name—custodiaphobia.'

I still stared down.

'Lots of kids have fears,' the Clodd said now. 'Even the biggest toughest kids are scared of SOMETHING. Toughest kid at my old school turned out to be scared of velvet.'

Now it was the Clodd who was staring at the big

knot in the summerhouse bench. 'I know another kid who's scared of custard,' she said. And a sad sort of look crept over her sharp pointy face—I had no idea why. 'She has nightmares about it.'

Then she looked at me, and narrowed her eyes. 'So, the fear. . . how was it you got it?' she said. 'Watching clowns at the circus? Was that what did it? Seeing them covered in custard pies? That's how the kid I know got it. She was terrified. Of the clowns *and* of the custard.'

I shivered again. Then sat there, breathing deeply. 'I do NOT talk about it,' I said.

'Suit yourself,' the Clodd said, shrugging.

And, for some reason—maybe because the Clodd looked like she didn't care if I told her or not, I found myself telling her.

'If you *must* know,' I said, 'something happened to me, a horrible CUSTARDY something—back when I was four.'

I was staying with my cousin, Milo, when it happened.

Milo's dad—my uncle—is Charlie. Boss of *Charlie's Colossal Cakes*. He has a big bakery, making cakes. Big cakes. Small cakes. Novelty cakes. All sorts of cakes, all shapes and sizes.

And that day, Milo hatched a plan for me and him to sneak into the bakery, next door to Milo's house, and help ourselves to some cupcakes.

I did NOT want to do it. I knew it was wrong, and I was scared of being caught. So I said no...

Milo ignored me. He said I had to do it. And as Milo was a year older, and bigger and stronger than me—in the end, I did.

So Milo sneaked us into the bakery, and up on to a big iron walkway, with big iron railings.

I remember, clear as clear, staring down. Seeing cakes everywhere, rows of cakes going along conveyor belts. Cakes being iced. Cakes being packed.

Seeing machines, big machines—all stamping and swirling and punching and spinning.

Seeing grown-ups, lots of grown-ups, wearing blue overalls, with nets over their hair—all scurrying about, looking busy.

And right below us—a big row of containers.

Vast metal containers, giant containers. All full of things bubbling and churning, and waiting to be turned into cakes.

Then one of the grown-ups looked up. She spotted us, and started shouting and pointing.

I panicked, and Milo panicked more. He told me

to run—but I knew running was wrong and useless. Running would just get us in more trouble. They had spotted us, they knew who we were. So I said no...

Milo ignored me *again*. He FORCED me to run. Dragged me after him, back along the walkway with its big iron railings. Railings designed to keep grown-ups safe...

*Not* designed to keep a four-year-old safe.

And, as Milo dragged me, I tripped—and toppled straight through the railings.

Down and down and down I fell. Closer and closer and closer to a big gloopy vat of chilled CUSTARD...

'They pulled me out pretty quick,' I told the Clodd. 'But even so—I'll never forget it. The shock...'

I shuddered. 'The squelching... the squerching... the floundering in custard...'

The Clodd shuddered too. 'Euggh...' she said.

'I stayed in hospital that night,' I said. 'And after that—I never did another one of Milo's plans. Never. From then on—we only did *my* plans.'

Which was true.

Because next morning Milo came to see me. Looking shocked and guilty. He brought me a card he had made to say he was sorry. Then he told me he had a much better, safer plan for today.

I said no. In fact—I gnashed my teeth and yelled at him. I yelled no, and that I was not doing any of his plans. Not EVER again. From now on, I was only doing *my* plans. And so was he.

And, somehow, overnight, things changed between me and Milo. Because he took one look at me, gnashing my teeth, and yelling at him—and he agreed. And that's what we've done ever since.

'Hm,' said the Clodd, looking thoughtful. 'Hm...'

I stared. *Hm?* First Bill, now her. What did the Clodd's *hm* mean?

I found out.

'That sort of explains it,' said the Clodd, nodding her head up and down.

'Sort of explains what?' I said grumpily. Because the Clodd was peering at me like she was a scientist, and I was some strange little specimen in a jar.

'You being such an idiot,' the Clodd said.

I half-gaped, half-glared.

'So... the custard incident...' she said, nodding. 'That's where the control thing started. You controlling Milo—to keep safe from any MORE custard incidents.'

Now the Clodd was nodding again. 'Then...

somehow—being the idiot you are,' she said, 'you did the same with ALL kids. Doing things *your* way to keep you safe. Even though the chance of another custard incident is round about zero.'

I spluttered. What a RIDICULOUS idea. The Clodd was wrong. Utterly wrong.

Doing things my way was *nothing* to do with fear of another custard incident. I did things my way because my way was BETTER.

But the Clodd was still nodding. 'Yes,' she said. 'Probably trauma… Shock… The custard incident. That's what turned you into an idiot.'

And she *still* hadn't finished. 'Then your mum and dad—all the new walls,' she said, 'that's made you even WORSE. Even MORE determined to be in control with Bill. With kids. Because you've got no control over the grown-ups.'

She looked at me. 'That's it,' she said, nodding more. 'You were already an idiot because of the custard. But your mum and dad, all the walls, they made you *more* of an idiot.'

'Will you STOP calling me an idiot?' I said, grinding my teeth.

'Course,' she said, standing up. 'Soon as you stop being one. Especially with Bill.'

Then she gave me an annoying sort of half-smile and a pat on the head. 'Cheer up,' she said. 'You may be an idiot—but it's curable. You don't have to *stay* an idiot. Not for ever and ever. All you have to do is let Bill be Bill.'

**18**

I sat there in the summerhouse, seething. Let Bill be Bill—what did the Clodd *mean*? Who ELSE would Bill be?

And she called me an idiot. Again. Well, she was wrong. It was the Clodd who was the idiot, NOT me.

And now she was having a kickabout—with Lekeisha. *And* Harriet. *And* Errol. I felt my teeth grind, just looking at the four of them. All of them, RUINING things.

Then I had a thought. Maybe *I* should ruin things for them. Ruin their kickabout. But how?

And—just like that—a plan popped into my head.

I started to chuckle. Because, right behind the summerhouse was the school garden. A walled garden, behind a locked door, to stop kids sneaking in...

So I boggled my way into the garden.

It was deserted, like I knew it would be. Just me, the flowerbeds—and the *chickens*.

The chickens were new last term. A lady came to our school and gave a talk in assembly, all about chickens and chicken care. Then she gave us four chickens to keep.

Buff Orpingtons, they're called. All pale goldy-brown, with little red heads. And, the lady said, excellent chickens for children—because they have a calm and friendly temperament.

Well... most of them.

But NOT Esmerelda. She's a moody sort of chicken. Just right for the job I had planned.

So I shot across the garden. 'Esmerelda,' I said. 'Esme, come here.' Then I opened the gate into the chicken run.

Esmerelda looked up at me, and clucked in an irritated sort of way.

I crouched down. 'You, Esme,' I told her, 'are about to make history. The first—and ONLY—wallboggling chicken in the world!'

Then I picked her up carefully, the way the lady showed us...

Esmerelda tried to peck my finger off.

She started struggling. She struggled and struggled, all the way from the chicken run to the garden wall. She pecked, she twisted, she clucked, pecked again. Trying her hardest to escape.

But I held her tight as I could. Stood by the garden wall. Stared at the wall and focused. Tried to ignore Esmerelda, struggling and clucking in my arms. Tried not to wonder if it would actually *work*...

It was tricky. Harder to focus. And it took longer to do because of Esmerelda. But—at last—me and Esmerelda boggled our way through both walls and into the summerhouse.

Esmerelda did *not* like the experience of being a wallboggling chicken. Not one bit. She wriggled and squirmed, so I put her down on to the ground. And she stood there, clucking up at me. In a VERY bad mood indeed.

Then she turned, and took a run at the wall we had just boggled through. Headbutted it—then staggered away, dazed. And went for a big peck at my leg.

I turned her around, so she was facing out into the playground.

'Not me,' I said. 'Them!' Then I gave her a small push of encouragement.

A small push was all she needed.

Clucking angrily, Esmerelda hurled herself out of the summerhouse, and straight into the kickabout. A furious, indignant sort of chicken. A *rampaging* chicken. Threatening and pecking wherever she could...

At Lekeisha. At Harriet. At Errol. And then, at the Clodd.

I sat myself down on the summerhouse bench and watched them—all screeching and yelling, all hopping about, clutching at their pecked legs.

I chuckled more. My plan could *not* have gone better. And now, there was pandemonium all over the playground. Kids running, shrieking and terrified, from the rampaging Esmerelda. Teachers swarming towards her, trying to catch her…

And here came the Clodd. Hopping over to me in the summerhouse. She showed me the peck on her leg. Then folded her arms and stared at me, eyes glinting. 'So… the chicken thing,' she said. 'Pointless plan number two.'

She sat down next to me. 'I know you did it,' she said. 'It had to be you. And I know why. Because I pointed out the fact you're an idiot.'

I glared. She ignored me.

'So… Is it shrinking?' she said. 'Is that how you did it? Are you a shrinker? Did you shrink yourself? Shrink yourself as tiny as an ant and get through some little crack in the wall?'

Now, that was clearly ridiculous. And the Clodd had to be told.

'If a kid could—just *suppose*—' I said, 'shrink itself tiny as an ant… How could it carry a CHICKEN?'

'Good point,' said the Clodd thoughtfully.

Then those conker eyes of hers lit up. 'Ah, *but*…' she said, jabbing me with a finger, 'if you could shrink yourself AND shrink the chicken—that would do it. So is that what you do? Shrink things? Yourself and other things?'

Now she grabbed my arm. 'Shrink me,' she said. 'I'd like a go at being shrunk. I'd like an ant's-eye view of things.'

'I am not a shrinker,' I snapped. 'Now leave me alone.'

That afternoon Mr Franklin had a plan for creative writing. 'Cutlass Class,' he said. 'You are going to write a diary entry. Each table working together, as a team. Planning. Discussing.'

I felt myself slump. Me and the Clodd writing a diary entry? *Together?* As a team? Planning? Discussing? Would this day NEVER end?

A day in the life of an olden-days child from Craggelton… That was what Mr Franklin wanted the diary entry to be.

Because we've been studying diaries—famous

diaries—in history. How they're a good way to find out about the past, and how real people lived.

And we've also been studying olden-days children here in Craggelton. Actual real-life kids. A boy chimney sweep who got sent to Australia as a criminal for stealing a gold ring. A girl who disguised herself and went to sea as a cabin boy...

But I knew straight away which kid we were writing about. So I told the Clodd.

'Drummond Moraggon,' I said. 'We're writing a day in *his* life.'

'Drummond Moraggon?' said the Clodd. 'Who's he, then?'

'A twin,' I said, 'with Morwenna Moraggon. And *I* live where their house, Moraggon Manor, used to be. So we're writing about Drummond Moraggon.'

The Clodd just sat there, eyes glinting. 'Is that what you call discussing?' she said.

'Yes,' I said.

She stared more. And now, a strange thing was happening. Something about the way the Clodd was sitting there—just staring, not speaking—was making me feel a bit... well, *foolish*. And I did NOT like feeling foolish, so I glared at her.

As usual, she ignored me.

'Suppose I want us to do a day in the life of Morwenna Moraggon, not Drummond?' she said now. 'I *might* want to. And we are supposed to be DISCUSSING.' And her eyes glinted more.

I got a strange feeling. The Clodd... was she *laughing* at me? No. Surely not. She couldn't be. Why would she be laughing at me? What was there to laugh about?

In the end, the Clodd *forced* me to do a shared diary. We did different handwriting for the two of them. The Clodd did Morwenna and I did Drummond.

We wrote about them being tutored at Moraggon Manor in the morning. Then helping the grown-ups finish building the secret wreckers' tunnel in the afternoon. Then arguing at bedtime, and setting off the Craggelton poltergeist. Then waking up in the night to a storm and a shipwreck, and charging through the wreckers' tunnel to get the loot.

It was an action-packed diary to write. With pictures. And the Clodd had no time to be annoying while we were doing all that... Until we finished.

Because, as we both sat back, proud of our shared diary entry, the Clodd said this. 'See?' she said. 'You did a whole afternoon—well, *almost*—without being an idiot. There is hope for you yet.'

And I felt my teeth start to grind. How could one kid be *so* annoying?

But there was something annoying me even MORE than the Clodd. Because it was now over TWO WHOLE DAYS that I had been a wallboggler. And Bill *still* didn't know.

## 19

I read more of Matilda Arkle's Book of Secrets that night...

*My governess has a* SECRET GENTLEMAN FRIEND! *For I saw them — my governess and Lord Futterbungle — canoodling in the orchard.*

*Later, I confronted her with my knowledge.*

*Oh, how she begged for my silence. For my father has* EXPRESSLY FORBIDDEN *servants to canoodle with visiting guests.*

*'I will lose my position,' she pleaded. 'My livelihood. Please do not tell.'*

*How swiftly I spotted an* OPPORTUNITY!

*'I shall keep your secret,' I told her. 'But in return, I ask one thing...'*

*And thus, tomorrow — I shall be* RID *of this stuffy old schoolroom.* RID *of this big dull house.* RID *of* the tall dark trees that surround it like guards, and block all views of the world beyond!

And RID of Lavinia. For my governess has informed my father that fresh air and new views are an invigorating tonic for the brain of a child. And so she and I shall be visiting a place I have longed to visit. The SEA!

I shall not sleep a WINK tonight!

I read on, all about her trip to the sea…

The sea is the stuff of my DREAMS. And those views, those far views! Of the sparkling sea, and the horizon—so full of promise, of ADVENTURE!

And now, dear Book, for my GREATEST of secrets!

I have found the spot where I will—one day—build myself a HOUSE. A fine sturdy house. High up on a hilltop, overlooking the sea, and the huge wide WORLD!

For now, the spot is a sorry sight. Desolate, neglected. Full of charred remains. All that is left of a burnt-down manor, built, it is rumoured, by wreckers. A spot where none will build—for it is said to be haunted. Haunted by an evil spirit—a tormentor of children, a bringer of fear…

*Pah! I have no such fear.*
*THIS is the place I shall build!*

I closed the Book of Secrets, and headed for the cellar stairs, amazed.

So... that trip to the sea—it was to *Craggelton*. And Matilda Arkle had stood, as a child, on the burnt remains of the old Moraggon Manor. Staring out to sea, with a plan in her head...

To build again. To build here, on this very spot. To build Ivy Lodge.

I could hear voices in the sitting room as I came up the stairs. So I thought it would be safe to take a shortcut—by boggling straight through the cellar wall and into the kitchen.

It *wasn't* safe.

Because there was Isabel. Standing at her easel, painting smock on, dabbing a paintbrush at a swirly splodgy mess.

I was shocked—and so was Isabel. Her mouth dropped open as she saw me boggle my way into the kitchen.

Her paintbrush clattered on to the kitchen floor. 'Ned, can you do MAGIC?' she gasped, eyes popping.

'Course,' I said, thinking quickly. 'Can't you?'

She thudded over and grabbed my arm.

'Teach me,' she ordered. 'Teach me to walk through the wall.'

'Can't,' I said, walking towards the stairs. 'Only boys can do magic. Only boys can make their eyes go all starey and then walk straight through the wall. NOT girls.'

BIG mistake—because before I was halfway up the stairs, I heard yells from downstairs. Yells from the kitchen. The piercing yells of a four-year-old.

I ran downstairs just as Mum and Grace rushed into the kitchen.

I rushed after them—and there was Isabel, bawling by the kitchen wall, with a big bump on her head.

'Grace,' said Mum. 'Frozen peas. Quick!'

Grace ran to the freezer, Mum ran towards Isabel—and Isabel started yelling. 'Is there *blood*?' she yelled. 'Is there BLOOD?'

'Just a bruise,' Mum said, grabbing the frozen peas off Grace and pressing them to the bump. 'But... what did you do? How did you get such a big bump?'

'I walked into the wall!' Isabel yelled. Then she swivelled and looked at me, standing in the doorway.

'It was Ned's fault,' she said, pointing her short

fat finger at me, blue eyes blazing. 'He should have TEACHED me to walk through walls. Then I wouldn't have a such ILL head!'

Now Mum and Grace both started staring, eyes goggling, at Isabel. 'To walk through *walls*?' Mum said, faintly.

'Yes!' bellowed Isabel. 'Ned walked through the wall! He did! The kitchen wall! And Ned said only *boys* can walk through walls. But my teacher said girls can do EVERYTHING boys can do. So I tried!'

Mum leant forward, and clutched Isabel's hand.

'Isabel, listen to me,' she said, looking worried. 'Did you try to walk through the wall because you are SAD about the walls? Because you want the walls *gone*?'

'NO,' said Isabel. 'I like them. You and Daddy don't do shouting now. Only Ned is sad about the walls. And he can walk through them!'

Grace was looking at Isabel, stunned. 'Wow,' she said, still goggling. 'That is some imagination!'

'Ned,' bellowed Isabel. 'Tell them you did it. TELL THEM! Tell them your foot camed through the wall, then all of you!'

I shook my head sadly. Then I leant forward. 'What about other walls?' I asked Isabel. 'Can I stick my foot through them? Or is it just that wall?'

Isabel gaped at me. 'Why are you asking *me*?' she said. 'I am a LITTLE GIRL. How do *I* know what walls you can walk through?'

Now Mum was looking at Isabel with a VERY worried expression. So I turned to Mum and did some shaking of my head.

'Delicate mechanism, the brain of a four-year-old,' I said. 'Probably short-circuiting because of all these new walls. Better call the doctor.'

Then I sauntered off upstairs.

Isabel stomped upstairs a few minutes later, and stood in my doorway, hissing like a small angry serpent.

'You fibbed,' she hissed. 'You said I was making it up. But I *know* you did it.'

Then she folded her arms. 'I am NOT your friend,' she said. 'And I am going to my bedroom, and I will sit and WAIT. And you think about what you have *done*. And when you are ready to SAY SORRY—you come and *see me*!'

Then she stomped off.

Now, I just have to say here, I am NOT proud of what I did next. It was mean. It was horrible. But I did it.

Because my room is right next to Isabel's—with only a wall between us . . .

So I boggled through the wall to see her. 'I am NOT

sorry,' I said, as Isabel sat there, eyes popping. 'And, yes, I *can* walk through walls—but NO ONE will believe you.'

Then I boggled back through the wall.

I waited a few seconds, then I stuck my head through the wall, and beamed at Isabel. 'Oops,' I said. 'My mistake. Wrong bit.'

I pulled my head back, then stuck my right arm through, and gave her a wave. Then I stuck a leg through, and waggled it about. And then—all of me went through.

Isabel glared as I stood there, grinning at her.

'That is ACTUAL bullying,' she said, wagging her finger. 'And I am telling. But Mummy is out getting pizza. So I am telling *Grace.*'

Which meant Grace came to see me a few minutes later. And now it was her standing in my doorway—and she was making the hissing noise too. Like a bigger angry serpent.

'I have *no idea* what's going on with you and Isabel,' she hissed. 'But it's mean to keep pretending you can walk through walls.'

'I *can* walk through walls,' I said. 'It's just not the kind of thing you tell a mum.'

Grace's jaw dropped.

'And it's not just the one wall,' I said. 'It's all walls. Indoor, outdoor. All kinds. Wood, brick, pebble-dash. The whole lot.'

Grace started hissing more. So I shook my head sadly.

'I can't win,' I said. 'First you hiss at me for *pretending* I can walk through walls. Now you're hissing at me for admitting I *can*.'

The hissing noise got louder. And I watched as Grace left, slamming my door behind her.

**20**

Bill was back in school that Friday. Standing in the middle of the playground when I arrived—handing out invites. Party invites...

I knew Bill was having a party this Saturday, four days before his actual birthday. And I knew where. At Rival Wreckers Run—a paintballing place me and Bill went to once before. What I didn't know was just how many kids he was inviting...

I stood there dazed. Counting.

Five... Six... Seven... How many invites was Bill giving out?

Ten. Bill gave out TEN party invites in the end. Not just to Lekeisha, Harriet, Errol, the Clodd... But to Ollie, Maisie, Josh...

On and on.

Then Bill spotted me—and a look flitted across his face. A wary, shifty sort of look. NOT the sort of look a best friend should have.

I forced myself to stay calm. I knew, just from that look—Bill's thinking was still *hopelessly* muddled. Well, today I would UNmuddle him. At the Tower Two meeting.

But first, I had to make SURE it happened. So I stretched my mouth into a big grin, and gave Bill a cheery wave.

Bill's eyebrows shot up. He looked surprised. Then I walked over to him, the grin still stretched across my face.

Remember the Tower Two meeting, I told myself. NOTHING must stand in its way.

'Ned,' said Bill, handing me an invite. 'This is for you.'

I ripped it open...

### BILL'S BIRTHDAY PARTY!
*This Saturday!*
*Rival Wreckers Run!*
*Party tea and games!*
*Shivery seaside stories by torchlight!*

'Thank you,' I said, putting on the happiest, most thrilled voice I could manage.

'I did invite quite a few other kids,' Bill said—and *his*

voice was sounding a bit nervy. And there it was again, the wary, shifty sort of look. As if he expected me to be cross.

Well, I *was* cross. But only secretly. Because I *needed* this Tower Two meeting. So…

'Good idea,' I said. 'The more the merrier.'

I didn't think that, of course. Not at all. But I had a feeling Bill would *like* me to say that. So I did, for the sake of the meeting.

Bill's eyebrows shot up again. 'You think it's a good idea?' he said.

'Totally,' I said.

I didn't think Bill could look more astonished, but he did. 'So… you don't mind?' he said.

'Absolutely not,' I said. 'You can have more than one friend. In fact, I think it's *good* if you have more than one friend.'

'Oh…' said Bill, and now he had a dazed sort of look.

I started nodding hard. 'Because I—who saved your actual life—will always be your *best* friend,' I said. 'And you having some other friends does NOT make you a worse friend to me.'

I was lying. All of it, total lies. But I had a feeling it was the sort of lies Bill wanted to hear.

Now Bill started nodding. 'I *do* want to be your friend, Ned,' he said. 'But I think it has to be a bit more ... equal. I think it would be a better friendship that way.'

It was hard. So SO hard. But I managed to nod. 'Totally,' I said.

Then I paused. Because *this* was the important bit. The ONLY bit that mattered.

'And—as equals,' I said, 'shall we have that Tower Two meeting at dinnertime?'

I had to keep it up ALL MORNING. Nodding and agreeing with Bill. Ignoring the Clodd, who was sitting there, eyes narrowed as she looked at me.

Then—*at last*—it was almost dinnertime.

I sat there, watching the clock. Five minutes ... four ... three ... two ... one ...

RRRRRRRRRRRRRRRING!

The dinnerbell rang out—and Mr Franklin held up his hand. 'Cutlass Class,' he said. 'Collect one of these on your way out.'

Then he waved a piece of paper. I knew what it was straight away. Clubs list. A list of all the after-school clubs for this year.

I got my clubs list and stared down. And there it was—Table Tennis Club.

I jabbed Bill in the side. 'Look,' I said, pointing, as we left the classroom. 'This year we're going to be the WINNERS! Top of the league!'

Because Table Tennis Club has a league table, with matches each week. And last year we were beaten to top place by Adam and Errol. Just.

But Bill was frowning. And with a horrible HORRIBLE lurch—I realized why.

Table Tennis Club was after school on Thursdays...

The same day as *bouldering*.

Panic flooded through me. Sheer panic. I grabbed Bill's arm. 'Bouldering—' I said, shaking my head. 'You can't do it.'

Bill stood there, frowning. 'But I want to do it,' he said. 'I like bouldering. I'm good at it. I think I *should* do it.'

I stared at him. 'And I think you should NOT,' I said. 'Not if it's Thursdays.'

Now Bill scratched his head. 'I *do* want to do table tennis,' he said. 'But I think I want to do bouldering MORE.'

I grabbed Bill's arm. How could Bill's thinking be *so* confused? Bouldering—more important than Table Tennis Club?

No, no, NO.

'Bill,' I said. 'If you do bouldering, then we have NO CHANCE of being table tennis champions!'

Bill started shaking his head. 'I think it's just *me* who has no chance of being table tennis champion,' he said. '*You* still have a chance—because you could be table tennis champion with someone else.'

I felt anger stirring inside me. How could Bill be missing the point so COMPLETELY?

So…

'You can NOT do bouldering!' I said—well, more sort of barked, right in his face. 'Choose! You have to *choose*! Who is your best friend? Me or Lekeisha? And who is it who SAVED YOUR ACTUAL LIFE on Sunday?'

It was no use. Bill got a stubborn sort of look on his face. Then he stuck his chin out.

'I don't think I have to choose,' he said. 'Not between friends. I think I have to choose between *activities*.'

I felt my teeth grind. Was Bill *never* going to understand the right thing to do? It was simple. So why didn't he just do it?

Well, there was only one thing to do. Explain his choices, so clearly that even Bill couldn't FAIL to understand.

'Bill,' I said. 'If you choose me and Table Tennis Club on Thursdays—I will tell you my secret. The biggest secret the Tower Two has EVER had!'

Bill stared. 'The biggest secret the Tower Two has ever had?' he said slowly.

'Yes!' I said.

Then I paused. So Bill could be absolutely sure to understand.

'*If*, however...' I said, 'you choose Lekeisha and bouldering on Thursdays—you will never EVER hear my secret.'

Then I stood there and folded my arms. That should do it. Sort this whole mess out.

It didn't. Bill just stuck his nose in the air—as if I was being completely unfair. When I wasn't.

'I think a true friend would tell me the secret anyway,' he said. 'Whatever I choose to do.'

Then he folded his arms too, and stared straight at me.

I backed away—just a bit. Bill had a stern sort of look on his face. What was that doing there?

'I have been doing a LOT of thinking these past few days,' Bill said now. 'And what I think is this. That you are being unreasonable and selfish.'

I gaped. The CHEEK of it. Bill, talking to me like that. *Me!* How dare he?

I felt my face flush bright red. I felt my teeth start to gnash. I felt rage, fury, panic—all at once—all whooshing right through me.

'Since you are so keen to tell me your thinking,' I hissed, 'even though it is, as usual, ALL WRONG—I am now going to tell you MY thinking. Which is *this*. That you are a *traitor*! A traitor to the Tower Two, a traitor to me, and a traitor to our friendship!'

Then I fumbled in my pocket. Dragged Bill's invitation out. Waved it in front of his face.

'And I also think *this*,' I hissed. 'That you are NO friend of mine! And that there is only one place IN THE WORLD for this!'

Then I ripped the invitation in two, marched across the playground—and shoved it right in the bin.

**21**

After school I stomped off to the beach. Sat myself on a rock near the top of the sand, and stared gloomily out to sea.

Why oh why oh why was it so HARD being a kid? Why couldn't I be a bit of sea? Because the sea doesn't care about *anything*. It just IS. Just does what it does. Comes in. Goes out. Gets stormy. Calms down.

And that would be easier—WAY easier—than being a boy. Than being *me*. Stuck with Bill for a friend...

An EX-friend.

I thought about Saturday. About Bill, all the other kids, at Rival Wreckers Run. The fun they'd have there. Running about in all the protective gear—the helmet, the goggles, the overalls—hiding, ambushing, leaping out to splatter each other with paint.

Yes, all that fun I'd be missing. All because of Bill. It was ALL Bill's fault. Bill and his stupid stupid bouldering.

But—oh no—that annoying niggle was *back*.

Interrupting my thinking. *Are you* sure *it's all Bill's fault?* the niggle was going. *Are you* sure?

Well, there was only one way to deal with that niggle. I IGNORED it. *Completely*. And I sat there, feeling cross. More than cross. Cross and *upset*.

Then I heard footsteps behind me. Clompy footsteps.

I turned and scowled.

The Clodd ignored me and sat down. 'You know what?' she said. 'The Bill thing . . . It is actually *you* who is at fault here. Demanding he does table tennis. Ripping up the party invite.'

I glared at her. 'It's not ME at fault,' I said. 'It's Bill.'

The Clodd just stared at me. Saying nothing.

I felt fed up. Because the Clodd was doing it *again*. Making me feel foolish. And, even worse—all her staring was setting off that annoying niggle.

So, once more, I crushed the niggle down. Then I stared down at my trainers, so I didn't have to see those conker eyes glinting at me.

It *was* Bill's fault. It WAS.

'Another thing,' she said. 'Sharing a table with two kids who give each other the glares all afternoon is NOT my idea of a good time. So you could grovel to Bill. Apologize. Put things right.'

I felt myself spluttering as I looked at the Clodd. ME? Grovel to *Bill*? Apologize? Put things right?

As if...

'And stop scowling,' she said. 'Bill's right. There's plenty of other kids you could do table tennis with. Like me.'

'YOU?' I said.

'Why not?' she said. 'You're an idiot, but I can cope. And if you're any good—well, so am I. We'd have a chance.'

I'd heard enough.

'When I want your opinion I will let you know,' I snapped. 'But I WON'T want it. Ever. About anything.'

I stood up. So did the Clodd.

Then I spotted something—a shape in the distance. A wiry, speedy shape. Heading along the prom.

'Quick!' I hissed at the Clodd. 'Hide!'

I grabbed her arm and hurtled down the sand and behind a big rock. 'Not a word,' I hissed, crouching down. 'Don't even breathe. Not until he's gone.'

All credit to the Clodd—she got it straight away. She crouched, making herself small as possible, just the way *Secret Sleuth* showed.

I held my breath. Peeked out from behind the rock. What was Snapper doing? He was walking along the sand, towards the sea. I got a glimpse of his face, all twitchy and nervy. And his eyes—staring, determined, scanning around for something...

Then he stooped. Picked up a piece of seaweed, long and thin, all in strands. Then another—fat, with bobbly bits on it.

Nothing odd about that—Snapper was always picking up things from the beach. But he was staring hard at them both, a big grin on his face. And a horrible thought popped into my head...

Did he have some sort of sneaky plan for that seaweed?

Then, with a flash of trainers, he went speeding back along the beach and on to the prom.

The Clodd got to her feet. 'So,' she said. 'Who was that?'

'Snapper,' I said. 'My one-time friend—but no longer. Likes ambushing kids. Especially me and Bill.'

Then I showed her the purple bruise all over the back of my arm. 'See that?' I said. 'Snapper did it. He shoved me into a wall.'

The Clodd raised her eyebrows. '*Another* one-time friend?' she said. 'Making a bit of a habit of it, aren't you?'

I didn't even bother to reply. I just gave the Clodd the biggest glare I could, and headed up the beach.

Back home in my bedroom, I could NOT stop brooding about Bill. Feeling crosser and crosser and crosser. Then I heard a car coming through the front gates.

A visitor. Who for? Mum? Or Dad?

I looked out of the window as the car door opened, and the visitor got out. A tall man with wavy hair...

I felt my mouth drop open.

Mr Franklin. *He* was the visitor? But what was he doing here?

Then I heard the front door bell ring. The dad-bell...

Quick! I boggled my way into the dad-side, tiptoed along the landing, and crouched at the top of the stairs.

Dad was showing Mr Franklin towards the sitting room. And Mum was there too. Dad *and* Mum? Together? Why?

So I tiptoed down the stairs, and listened at the door, just as Mr Franklin started speaking...

'I saw Ned ripping up a party invitation from William Egg at dinnertime,' said Mr Franklin. 'So I had a chat with him.'

Which he did.

Mr Franklin called me inside, and sat me in the

classroom. Then he asked me why I had done it. So I explained about Bill doing bouldering on Thursdays with Lekeisha when he should be doing table tennis with me.

I explained all about it—and, for some reason, Mr Franklin sighed. Then he started asking questions.

'Ned,' he said. 'What do you think makes a good friend?'

So I told him. 'Bill,' I said. 'The way he used to be.'

I saw a frown furrow its way across Mr Franklin's brow. As if he didn't think that was the right answer. Which it was.

'And how would you describe your friendship with Bill?' Mr Franklin asked me after that. 'In three words?'

I thought. 'Messed-up,' I said. 'That's with a hyphen— so it's only one of my words, not two. And annoying. And ruined.'

Mr Franklin nodded. 'And why do you think your friendship is messed-up and annoying and ruined?'

Well, that was easy. 'Because of Bill,' I said.

'Do you think it's ALL because of Bill?' said Mr Franklin.

'Yes,' I said.

Which got Mr Franklin sighing again—just like he

was sighing now to Dad and Mum. Even though *that* was the right answer too. It WAS.

Although... nooooo! That niggle was back. *Are you sure it was the right answer?* the niggle went. *Are you sure it's all because of Bill?*

That niggle was getting ON MY NERVES, and I wanted it gone. I tried to crush it down—but it was a PERSISTENT sort of niggle. It would *not* go.

On and on and ON it niggled.

'It seems Ned is struggling to understand how friendship works,' Mr Franklin said. 'He's a little... STUBBORN in his friendships. And in his dealings with his peer group.'

Well—I knew Mr Franklin was speaking English, but I had no idea what he was actually saying.

And now it was Dad who was sighing. 'Stubborn,' he said, 'is Ned's middle name.'

What? What did Dad mean? Why couldn't grown-ups speak *clearly*? Stubborn was NOT my middle name. Harrison was.

Now Mum joined in the sighing. 'The trouble with Ned,' she said, 'is once he gets an idea in his head, it's VERY hard to budge it. Poor aggravating Ned.'

I'd heard enough.

Dad and Mum insulting me. Mr Franklin talking

gobbledegook. I was NOT listening to any more. So I tiptoed back upstairs and through the wall, seething.

Aggravating—Mum called me *aggravating*. I was NOT aggravating. Because I know what aggravating means. It means troublesome, irritating, annoying, all the things Mum was. And Dad. And the sisters. And the Clodd. And Bill.

They were all aggravating. NOT me.

And I knew where I was going. Somewhere NO ONE aggravating could possibly find me. My secret den.

**22**

There was another notebook in the trunk. This one had a dark-green cover. And a label stuck on it...

*TOP SECRET!*
*CHILDREN ONLY!*

Top secret! I opened it up straight away. And stared at the first page...

*Trap-Setting: A Guide for Children*
*Begun, this Fourteenth Day of April*
*By Matilda Emmeline Arkle, aged Ten and One-Quarter*

Below the title she had stuck a photo. And written next to it...

*The Author, Aged Ten.*

I stared. It was a very old photo, a faded pale-brown sort of colour.

Matilda Arkle had lots of ringlets, and ribbons in her hair. She had frills on her dress and dainty shoes, ones with buttons on.

But she was standing in a very determined sort of way. And she had a look on her face that said hurry up and get this photo over with.

It was a sharp sort of face. Some small clues to the grown-up she'd become, the one in the portrait in the upstairs lobby. The fierce mouth. The staring eyes— eyes that gleamed out of the photo. Eyes that stared straight into mine. Eyes that seemed to see everything.

I turned the page, and started to read...

## Trap-Setting: An Introductory Note

*There is a fine art to the creation of traps.*
*A most excellent trap relies on balance and weight, on levers and pulleys, on choice of ingredients.*
*A child either understands these matters, or does not...*
*I do.*
*My first trap was some years ago, for Nanny—a monstrous old crone, with the snout of a warthog,*

*teeth rotted by time, and a distrust of ALL that a*
*child finds fun.*
*Daily, she would force upon me Drills.*

I stopped. Drills? Matilda got to use *drills*? To drill big holes, to build things? But... why was she so fed up about it? Drills sounded a LOT more interesting than flower arranging.

But then I read on.

Oh.

These sort of drills were different, not interesting at all...

*Drills — endless Drills. The dullest of exercises.*
*Marching, and arm swings, lunges, and stretches,*
*again and again.*
*And then, after Drills, give me MUTTON for dinner —*
*and the hardest of slaps when I spat the meat out.*
*My trap for Nanny was simple. One single ingredient —*
*flour, begged from Cook in the kitchen. Enough flour*
*to fill my small metal bucket. A bucket I wedged on*
*top of the part-open door to my nursery.*
*Although a simple trap, it had most pleasing results.*
*For Nanny pushed the door, the bucket tipped, the*
*flour fell — and Nanny shrieked as loud as a banshee.*

*Nanny packed her bags that very same day, and was GONE. The first of my nannies, but not the last.*

*And that was the day—a cold, frosty Friday—I discovered my skill. From that day on I have set traps for ALL who annoy me. Bigger traps, better traps, day by day.*

*Hence I write this guide so that others, too, may learn the fine art of trap-setting.*

*So read on, read on . . .*

I *did* read on. Because Matilda Arkle was a GENIUS. A brilliant trap-setter.

She spent a LOT of time setting traps. Traps for anyone who annoyed her—and most grown-ups did. *Especially* the nannies, then, later, the governesses.

She explained about using what she called Triggers and Releasings.

Triggers were things that caused a victim to trip. She had a list of Triggers—a long LONG list. A small pool of oil, a pile of tin tacks, a wire carefully placed to trip up a victim...

She had another long list too. This one of Releasings. Some I didn't know—like pottage and broth. But lots I did—like syrup and cream.

She explained how to think a trap through. How to

ask yourself questions. What happens when the Trigger gets its target? What will the victim do? Stagger sideways? Backwards? Fall to the floor? Where is the best place to put the first Releasing? The second? The third?

She explained how to picture it in your mind. How to set Triggers so the victim would stumble—helpless—as Releasings exploded all around.

She even drew diagrams. Detailed diagrams. Of indoor traps, of outdoor traps. And I stared at the diagrams. I stared and I stared. And a plan began to form in my head. A plan for Bill's party. A brilliant plan...

But now—a NEW niggle was starting up in my head. Is *it a brilliant plan?* the new niggle was saying. *Are you sure?*

I was FED UP with niggles. All of them.

So I stared at the photo of Matilda Arkle. I stared and I stared. And I thought about her words...

*From that day on I have set traps for ALL who annoy me.*

And I knew. Matilda Arkle would NEVER have a niggle in her head, asking annoying questions.

So...if Matilda Arkle would not have a niggle—then nor would *I*. Because it *was* a brilliant plan. It WAS.

\* \* \*

I heard Grace shrieking a bit later. Shrieking and shrieking.

I chuckled. Those shrieks meant Grace had just found my trap. My test trap. A simple two-parter, just to get the feel of things. Two tubs balanced over the bathroom door—one of water, one of flour...

Grace deserved it. Because earlier, when Mum came back with pizza. I grabbed my pizza off Mum. 'I am taking this to my room,' I said to Mum. 'Because bribing me with takeaway does NOT make the walls any better.'

And I was stomping off to the stairs when Grace shot out of the kitchen and grabbed me. 'You know what—' she hissed, 'the only person making things truly miserable around here is YOU.'

I just stuck my nose in the air and went off upstairs. But I did NOT enjoy eating my pizza alone in my bedroom. And that was ALL Grace's fault.

So she deserved a trap. And here she came, pounding up the stairs.

She barged in, dripping bits of flour and water, and plonked herself down on my bed.

'I don't believe I gave you permission,' I said.

'A trap,' she hissed. 'Why? WHY?'

I sat, not speaking, and watched Grace's teeth grind.

'All this, all the walls...' she hissed, glaring at me. 'You could help make this WORK!'

So I glared back. 'Why should I help?' I said. 'I don't *want* to make it work.'

'Don't you think Mum and Dad tried to stay together?' Grace said, hissing more. 'For ages and AGES? Don't you think they tried to split the best possible way they could?'

'I'm a kid,' I said. 'I don't have to think about things like that.'

Then Grace's phone gave a beep and she snatched it up and checked it. Straight off, her face went all scowly.

'Message from George?' I said.

'None of your business,' she snapped.

'He's going off you, I reckon,' I said. 'It's Friday night—where is he? Boyfriends *never* miss Friday night.'

'He's with his aunt,' snapped Grace. 'It's her BIRTHDAY.'

'Lying, probably,' I said. Then I shook my head and looked all gloomy. 'First love never lasts. Look at Mum—that hairy one in her photo album, the one with the bike. Her first love, she called him. Where is he now? History.'

Grace was going pale now.

'Reckon you're a sort of try-out,' I said. 'Like choosing a pet. Trying out all sorts until you find the one you like best. First a hamster, say. Then a cat—maybe a tabby. Then a spaniel... You're like the hamster. His first try-out.'

Grace gnashed her teeth. 'For your information,' she said, 'George is NOT going off me—and he bought me a present yesterday.'

She waved it in my face—a small plastic disc. A plectrum, for playing her guitar.

I shook my head. 'Boys in love don't buy plectrums, I reckon,' I said. 'They buy bunches of red roses. Or sparkling jewels.'

'It was a *thoughtful* present,' Grace said, teeth still gnashing.

'It was cheap,' I said.

Grace glared. 'What do YOU know about buying presents?' she hissed. 'You are the world's WORST present buyer.'

Then she shot off to her room—and a minute later, she shot back. 'You can have these back,' she said. 'They're rubbish.' Then she dumped some things on my bed...

**Itching Powder!**
**It's scratch-tastic!**

**Smelly slime!**
**A thousand uses!**

I stared down at them. It wasn't nice to be told that what I thought was the best present EVER was rubbish.

'Why would I want these?' Grace said. 'I'm a TEENAGER.'

Now *that* I could answer. 'I'll still want presents like that as a teenager,' I said.

'You, you, *you*,' Grace hissed. 'That's ALL you think about. That's all there's room for in Ned-world!'

Then she marched out of my room and slammed the door.

I had weird dreams that night. Weird worried dreams—
mainly running from wreckers, while the sky hailed
table tennis balls.

Then I woke, and it was Saturday. Handover day.
Time for mum-week to end, and dad-week to start.

So at half-past nine, me, and Isabel, and Mum—
not Grace, who was still asleep, and doesn't often
do weekend mornings—stood in the upstairs lobby.
Waiting.

Then we heard it. A key turning in the lock on the
dad-side. The dad-door opened—and there he was.

Dad.

I felt SO muddled.

Half-pleased, half-cross to see him. Half-wanting to
hug him, half-wanting to scowl. So I went for the scowl.

Unlike Isabel.

'Daddy!' she shrieked, hurling herself at him. She
tucked her hand in Dad's and skipped through the

dad-door. Then she turned and waved at Mum. 'See you in seven sleeps,' she beamed.

I turned to Mum—and felt muddled again. A hug or a scowl? I just didn't know. So I gave her a scowl too, and stomped into the dad-side.

'Presents first!' said Dad, handing out parcels. 'Moving-in presents!'

We ripped them open. An easel for Isabel to use in the dad-side, and new paints and brushes. And for me, two more *Secret Sleuth* books, plus a pair of drumsticks with a note attached.

Lessons start in two weeks.
Love Dad x

Drum lessons! I had been longing for them for a whole YEAR. But I felt all muddled again. One part of me wanting to run over and hug Dad. The other part still feeling cross.

So I went for the scowl again.

I knew I was being ungrateful. A bit of a brat. And I wouldn't have blamed Dad for cancelling the lessons. But he didn't. An upset sort of look flitted across his face. A look that made me feel guilty. So then I felt cross—cross with Dad for making me feel guilty.

Dad had plans for today... A trip to Craggelton lido. A huge outdoor saltwater pool—and one of my favourite places. With waterslides and rapids, and a big shipwreck in the middle.

'Swimming!' said Isabel. 'YES!' Then she started dancing round the kitchen, eyes shining, saying how *happy happy happy* she was it was dad-week.

But I felt even MORE muddled. I wanted to go. But I *couldn't* go. I had stuff to do. Stuff for my plan.

But—should I go anyway?

No. The plan was more important. So...

'Can't go,' I said. 'Stuff to do.'

'You sure?' Dad said, and the upset look was back, flitting across his face again. Which was not FAIR—because it made me feel guilty all over again. So I scowled even harder.

'TOTALLY sure,' I said, and marched out of the room.

Soon as Dad and Isabel left I started to get ready. Collecting up things I needed, stuffing them into my backpack. And, by the time Dad and Isabel got back, I was finished. Fully prepared.

We had lasagne for lunch, Dad's lasagne, made by him last night, specially for today. And Dad talked to me about Bill's party. Said he'd heard about me tearing up the invite. So I said yes, I had—but that me and Bill had made up this morning. And now I was going to his party.

It wasn't a complete lie.

Because I *was* going to Bill's party… just not as a GUEST.

I was here. Outside Bill's house, down the side alley, staring at the wall. Part-thrilled, part-terrified at what I was about to do. Then I focused, hard as I could, and took a step forward.

The house was empty, like I knew it would be, when I boggled my way in. Bill and his mum were at Rival Wreckers Run. And Bill's dad was away, working.

I went upstairs and into Bill's bedroom. Then stared, shocked.

Bill's room had changed. The wall of pictures—of him and me doing Tower Two stuff. It was gone.

Every single thing on his walls that reminded him of me.

GONE.

I was cross with Bill before, but now I felt *crosser*. Bill deserved this trap. Totally.

So I got busy, setting up the best trap I could. Adapting Matilda Arkle's ideas to fit Bill's bedroom, using the Triggers and Releasings I had managed to get hold of.

Then I hid. Because I was going to watch this trap happen. Every single SECOND of it.

I hid in the chest on Bill's landing—a big chest, wooden and strong. One me and Bill had often hidden in.

It's a comfy place to hide, half full of blankets. And it has a line of holes—circles—cut out along each side. A design feature, Bill's dad calls them. Spyholes, me and Bill call them.

I settled down to wait. I had a good view through the spyholes, of the top of the stairs, and the landing. And, most important of all—Bill's door, a bit ajar …

Then I heard a key in the lock, and here they all came. Trooping into the kitchen.

It was a LONG wait. I crouched in the chest, listening to the voices downstairs—the laughing, the yelling, the shouts. The party tea seemed to go on FOR EVER.

But—at last—they sang 'Happy Birthday' to Bill, and I could hear feet padding into the hallway.

I crouched lower. This was it! They were coming up here!

They weren't.

It was Bill's mum. Going out into the garden.

Then Bill started the party games in the sitting room. LOUD party games.

I started to fidget. The chest was *not* a comfy place any more. It was cramped, it was stuffy, and I was fed up.

When were they coming up here? *When?* Surely it HAD to be soon?

I had a horrible thought. Maybe they *wouldn't* come up here. Not until it was dark. Not until the shivery seaside stories. But… how late would that be?

I slumped down in the chest. Then, somewhere downstairs, a phone rang. And I heard feet running out of the sitting room, towards the stairs.

Up and up the feet came.

I peered out. It was the Clodd, on her phone, listening.

She sat down on the top step, looking worried. 'Ruby,' she said, sounding worried. 'Calm down.'

*Ruby?* Who was Ruby?

'Take a big breath, Ruby…' the Clodd was saying now. 'Yes, like when you jump in at the pool… And another… See? It helps with the crying. So now you can tell me what's wrong.'

There was silence from the Clodd after that. A long silence. Whoever Ruby was—she had a lot to say.

Then it was the Clodd's turn. 'Ruby, listen,' she said. 'It IS mean—but Sophie is *fibbing*. They NEVER eat little girls... Witches?... They might do... Yes, witches do taste of yuk, most probably...'

There was another pause. Then, 'She's fibbing again...' They're DEFINITELY real,' the Clodd said. '*All* towns have them... Keep looking—you might spot one...'

Another pause. 'Did you? *Another* nightmare?'

Now the Clodd's voice was cracking. 'Yes, I wish that too... More than ANYTHING. I do... Bye... Speak soon.'

Now Bill was coming up the stairs. 'Maddie!' he was calling. 'Maddie! We're starting the balloon game!'

The Clodd leapt to her feet, and backed away along the landing as Bill came up the stairs.

She was trying to smile. And failing. UTTERLY. Standing there, clutching her phone. With tears dribbling out of her eyes and down her cheeks.

Bill's mouth dropped open.

'Sorry,' she said, wiping the tears away and sniffing. 'It's just... that was my sister. Ruby. She's five.'

I crouched, astonished. The Clodd had a *sister*?

'She lives with Dad,' said the Clodd, with a gulp. 'Has done for a month.'

Bill stared, as astonished as I was. 'How come?' he said.

The Clodd sniffed again. 'Mum… Dad…' she said, 'They split up. Then Mum got a job here—a perfect job… Perfect except it's two hundred miles from Dad's job.'

Another big sniff from the Clodd. 'So they decided to share us. Have one of us each.'

*Share* them? That was the most RIDICULOUS thing I'd ever heard. Kids were not something you could share out, like a bag of Swizzlers. No, no, *no*.

More sniffing. 'So Ruby's in our old house with Dad, and I came here with Mum,' the Clodd said, miserably. 'And we'll meet in the holidays—but that's a LONG time away.'

I crouched there, head spinning. The Clodd, living with her mum… The sister, living with her dad…

Now the Clodd had more tears dribbling down her cheeks. She started to sniff—again and again. Then she wiped her hand across her face.

Bill took her arm. 'I don't think I have any WORDS that are useful,' he said, scratching his head. 'But I think I can BE useful. Because you need tissues, and I have a whole big box on my desk.'

'Thanks,' sniffed the Clodd.

It was like watching something in slow motion *and* speeded up, both at once.

Thoughts whipped through my brain as I watched. Bill taking the Clodd's arm and propelling her forwards... The Clodd, tears dripping down her face, missing her sister, her five-year-old sister...

And both of them, heading straight for Bill's bedroom door. Straight for my trap...

No. NO.

I pushed back the lid of the chest—and I jumped right out.

'Stop!' I yelled. 'Both of you—STOP!'

**24**

Too late. Bill was already pushing open his bedroom door and marching in...

He tripped, straight off. Tripped over a wire stretched across the doorway. Marbles started scattering all around him—and two tubs tumbled down from above the door. One of feathers, and one of green jelly.

The green jelly, freshly made this morning, splatted down on to Bill's head—and he went sprawling to the floor. Then he landed face first, in a bowlful of gloop.

He lay there, spreadeagled, as feathers fluttered and settled all around him. Then—slowly, slowly—he hauled himself to his feet. And turned around.

He stood there, dripping with gloop—flour mixed with water, and glitter, and raisins, and red paint—jelly sliding off his hair, feathers sticking to him all over.

He stood, staring straight at me. In silence. Utter silence. The Clodd right beside him.

I stood there too, frozen to the spot.

And now—there were footsteps, lots of footsteps. All the other kids, coming up the stairs. Lekeisha, Errol, Harriet, Ollie, Maisie, all of them...

All gaping at Bill, standing there, dripping.

Then gaping at *me*.

Bill took a step forward. Then another.

His face started flushing a dark dark red. His eyebrows started knotting. His teeth started gnashing. His fists started clenching and unclenching.

And, for the first time ever, Bill—who *never* gets angry, *never* loses his temper—started to ROAR.

'You!' roared Bill. 'YOU!'

Then he took another step towards me. Stood right in front of me...

I took a step back.

'You SNEAK into my house—I have *no idea* how,' he roared, 'and set a TRAP? A trap to *ruin* my party? The party I actually *invited* you to! You are an IDIOT! No—*worse* than an idiot. You're a NINCOMPOOP! An IMBECILE!'

I felt my knees wobbling. What had happened to Bill? Had he been replaced by an ALIEN? This wasn't the Bill I knew—not this red, roaring thing in front of me.

But it *was* Bill.

'You think I should STOP doing things I want to!' he

roared. 'You think I should NOT go bouldering. NOT make other friends. Because you think I should do what *YOU* want! Well, I think DIFFERENTLY!'

I backed away—towards the stairs . . .

But Bill grabbed my arm. Forced me to listen, as he roared on.

'Call yourself my FRIEND?' he roared. 'No! A friend is what you are NOT! Because a true friend would WANT me to do things I want to do. Not try and *stop* me!'

I stood there, legs wobbling. Bill looked like he was about to explode with anger, with FURY.

I started to panic. Could Bill *actually* explode? Was that possible?

Because if he did, then Bill exploding would be all my fault—and I'd never forgive myself. NEVER.

'Another thing,' Bill roared now. 'A true friend makes you HAPPY to be with. And you do NOT! You make me UNHAPPY!'

I tried to speak. But all that came out of my mouth was a mutter. 'Stop!' I muttered. 'Stop all the roaring. You've made your point. I'll go.'

Bill gnashed his teeth, right in my face. 'NO!' he roared. 'You stay right *here*! For once—it's your turn to LISTEN! Because you know what? You think you're right about everything. But you're NOT! You're WRONG!'

Now Bill started jabbing a finger at my front. 'You can do long-division sums faster than any kid in class… You understand how volcanoes work… You know most capital cities of the whole world…' he roared. 'But when it comes to being a friend—you know NOTHING! You are the most STUPID kid in Cutlass Class! In our school! In ANY school! Anywhere in the whole wide WORLD! In fact, there is not one kid on this whole PLANET who is as stupid as you about what it means to be a FRIEND!'

Then, all of a sudden—Bill stopped roaring. He gave me a glare. A terrible glare. Cold and hard, like his face was carved out of ice.

Then he spoke, in a voice to match. A cold hard voice, not like Bill's voice. Not at all. A voice full of, well… *contempt*. As if he could hardly be bothered to speak to me at all.

But he did speak.

'Get out of my house,' Bill said. 'RIGHT NOW.'

I *did* get out. I tried to be cross. Tried to tell myself Bill deserved the trap.

I failed. I was fooling myself. Bill did NOT deserve it. And he was right. What kind of kid did a TRAP to ruin a friend's party?

Me. That's who.

Ned Harrison Arkle-Smith...

So I trudged off home. I went the quicker way, up over the hills. I trudged through the whining gate, up along the footpath, shoulders drooping, feet dragging. Feeling miserable, feeling confused, feeling *ashamed*.

What a mess. What a total TOTAL mess...

High on the hills, I stopped. I could hear voices coming from the brick shelter. Voices, and sniggers. And sounds... *Spraying* sounds.

Then—out from the shelter came three kids. Bigger kids, MUCH bigger kids. The Hulk, and two of his mates, all swaggering out of the shelter, all holding cans of spray paint.

They sprayed one last big squirt each on the side wall—and that's when I realized what they were up to. Graffiti. Spraying the walls of the shelter with graffiti.

They spotted me and swaggered over, all three of them. Grouped themselves around me.

Then the Hulk smirked—right in my face. 'Ooh...' he said, pointing at the graffiti. 'Who could *possibly* have done that? Must have been the Craggelton poltergeist.'

His two friends sniggered. Then the Hulk stopped smirking and stared hard at me. 'You...' he said, speaking slowly and carefully, 'did NOT see that.'

He stared more. 'Get it?' he said.

I nodded. I couldn't help gulping. They were all so big, all sniggering, all staring.

Then the Hulk patted me on the head. 'Good boy,' he said. 'Now—run along.'

And I did. Fast.

No one was in when I got home. And I did NOT want to think about today, not any more. Not about Bill, or what I'd done.

So I went straight to my den. I opened Matilda Arkle's Book of Secrets, and started to read…

*Lavinia Montmorency is a MINX! At playtime yesterday I informed her what our game was to be. That we were to be travellers, riding camels across a hot desert in search of an oasis. That we were to meet marauding hordes, and take shelter behind the piano.*

*The wretched girl simply pursed her lips. 'But I want to skip,' she whined.*

*So I pinched her. 'Do as I say,' I told her, handing her the hobby horse.*

*Off she ran—sobbing once more—to our governess. And the withered old hag seized her chance. 'Thirty* lines,' she told me, chalking on the board, pleasure gleaming in her wicked eyes, 'of this!'...

Pinching is not an acceptable way for a young lady to settle a dispute.

Pah!
So this very day I had my REVENGE on Lavinia.
I whispered to her of the Hauntings — the tale I heard on my trip to the sea.
Whispered of that most VICIOUS of spirits. How it had preyed on the warring children of Craggelton. How it had haunted their days and their nights.
And Lavinia shivered and whimpered — just as I knew she would. For she once confided in me her deepest of secrets, her darkest of fears, the thing that most terrifies Lavinia in all of the world...
SPIRITS. Ghosts and phantoms and spirits.
Then I whispered more. That Lavinia should BEWARE. For the spirit had moved on from Craggelton — but to who knows where? That Craggelton was but twenty-five miles distant. That she should listen for knocking, for tapping, for banging noises. Signs that the spirit had moved on to US...

'NO MORE!' Lavinia begged, her face ashen. 'No more of this tale!'

I laughed, then I stamped on her foot.

Sobbing, she stamped on mine. And then — I pulled on a HIDDEN string to a HIDDEN trap. A trap I set last night. A fine, simple trap, hidden in my toy cupboard.

With one tug on the string my big box of marbles spilled on to the floor of my toy cupboard with a DEAFENING CLATTER.

'It is HERE!' I gasped, clutching Lavinia's arm, and flinging myself on a chair. 'It is inside my toy cupboard. It has come for us! For me, for YOU!'

How Lavinia shrieked! She shrieked and shrieked!

And how I laughed! I laughed so much I fell from my chair — as Lavinia ran screaming from the playroom.

I was shocked. That was mean. Really mean.

I thought about how terrified I felt, confronted by custard, the thing I feared most. How Lavinia must have felt, hearing the whispered tale of the Craggelton Hauntings, and the clatter of marbles in the toy cupboard.

Then I read on…

*Lavinia has GONE. She has asked to leave the schoolroom. From now on she will be studying with her cousin, Hortensia Spurgeon.*

*I demanded to know why.*

*Lavinia claimed my teasing was cruel and thoughtless. I replied it was necessary. To teach her never again to go sobbing to our governess over the smallest of matters.*

*But did Lavinia understand this? She did NOT.*

*She says she will never return to my schoolroom. She says Hortensia Spurgeon is kind and caring, and would NEVER torment her.*

*To which I retorted that Hortensia Spurgeon sounded weak and dull—and well-suited to be Lavinia's companion.*

*And now, Lavinia's carriage has gone. Good riddance. I shall do a little dance for JOY.*

I sat and thought about Matilda Arkle. How I had liked her so much to start with. Admired her, even. But now this . . . this was no way for a kid to behave.

And I sat, and I thought. About Matilda and Lavinia . . . About me and Bill . . . About ways to do things differently. Ways to be a better, kinder friend.

I sat and I thought—and I wondered.

**25**

'Nooooo! Not like *that*! Like MUMMY does it!'

I could hear Isabel shrieking in the kitchen, from right up in my bedroom that evening. So I ran downstairs, and there she was—having a plaster put on by Dad. But not happy *at all* about the way Dad was doing it.

In fact, Isabel wasn't happy about anything. The shiny eyes of this morning were gone.

It was the walls—they were confusing her, all being in different places. She kept thinking she was in the mum-side when she wasn't. Going into the kitchen when she was looking for the toilet. Into the sitting room when she was looking for the kitchen…

And that plaster was for a scrape—a big one—on her knee, from a step she wasn't expecting.

It got worse when Dad made food. Isabel took one look at her plate, and started shrieking again.

'Not green and orange food on the SAME PLATE!'

she shrieked. 'And NOT TOUCHING! Mummy *never* does that!'

Then she tasted her omelette—and spat it out. 'Too EGGY!' she shrieked, just as the dad-door burst open, and Grace charged in and straight up the stairs to her bedroom.

I could hear Grace from my bedroom, two hours later. Sobbing.

I knocked on her door, but she didn't even answer. So I went in—and she leapt straight up and pushed me out again.

I only got a glimpse of her face. But a glimpse was enough. She looked miserable. Utterly miserable.

And Isabel did some sobbing too, at bedtime. Sobbing, then more shrieking. It took Dad more than an hour to calm her down. Then he had to arrange all her soft toys in her bed. And kiss them goodnight in turn, all eighteen of them.

She was asleep now—and I could hear voices downstairs. Two voices. Dad's ...

And Mum's.

So I crept towards the stairs, and listened.

'She's OK now, fast asleep,' said Dad. Then he gave a big sigh. 'Is this going to work, Laura? *Is* it?'

'I don't know,' said Mum. And *she* gave a big sigh. 'I just don't know. I think Isabel will get used to it—in time. Grace too. But Ned...'

She stopped. Sighed again.

'Ned's SO unhappy,' said Dad. 'So cross with all the walls. And with me. I saw him over the garden wall this week, and he yelled at me.'

I went cold.

Oh no. Not the yelling. Do NOT tell Mum about the yelling...

Because I was out in the garden, and I saw Dad's head. He was up a ladder, fixing something to the new wall between his bit of garden and Mum's.

And just seeing his head over the wall made my insides lurch. So I marched over and started yelling at him—how his head should NOT be visible in mum-week. How he should stay on his side of the wall, because I hated him. Then I yelled every single insult at Dad's head that I could—words I am NEVER allowed to use. Then I *spat*, as far and as high as I could, trying to get Dad right in the face.

But Dad didn't tell Mum any of that. He just sighed again.

Now it was Mum's turn. 'He did some yelling at me too,' she said. 'When I tried to help him with Ornflak.'

Oh no. Not Ornflak. Do NOT tell Dad about Ornflak…

Ornflak is a robot I built almost two years ago. Out of odds and ends, and cardboard cereal packets.

Mum and Dad both helped me build Ornflak. And once Ornflak was finished, he stood in a corner of my bedroom. Then, straight after they told me about the walls—I went off to my room and smashed him to pieces.

I regretted it straight away. Put all the Ornflak bits in a big box. But I never got round to mending him. So he's been in my cupboard all year.

'I found him looking at all the Ornflak bits,' Mum said. 'I offered to help with the rebuilding. Said I had some ideas. He said "no".'

Well—what I actually said was this: 'Get yourself OUT of my room.'

Then I started yelling at Mum. 'Ideas?' I yelled. 'You want to hear my ideas? You split the house—well, you can split us kids too. You can have Grace and Isabel, and Dad can have me! Because I HATE you!'

Now Mum was sighing. 'Ned wants to live with you,' she said. 'All the time. And for me to have Grace and Isabel.'

No… No. That wasn't true. I mean, yes—I *said* that. But I didn't *mean* it.

Now the two of them were sighing again. 'We thought the walls were such a good idea,' said Dad. 'The best way to do things.'

'It's a mess,' said Mum. 'I'm not sure it's working. The walls... you being so close... It just makes Ned muddled. *More* unhappy.'

'Should we sell Ivy Lodge?' said Dad. 'Get two smaller places? Would that be better? Less confusing?'

No. No more. I'd heard enough. I crept away.

Getting to sleep that night was hard. It was hot. Sticky. And thunder was rumbling, quiet low rumbles.

I lay in bed, tossing and turning. I tried counting imaginary goats leaping an imaginary gate into an imaginary meadow—which usually gets me to sleep. But not tonight.

My head was too full of thoughts. Muddled thoughts. Thoughts about Bill, about my family, about walls.

And thoughts about the Clodd, about something she'd said...

'*You've got no power over changes... The only power you have is how you deal with them.*'

Was the Clodd right? Was it time for me to deal with all those changes in a new way? A better way?

And those changes—with Bill, with the walls, were they all *really* so bad?

Was it so wrong for Bill to have new friends, new things to do? Or was it me who was wrong?

And the walls, were they there to keep my family apart... or TOGETHER?

I just didn't know.

And I had an aching sort of feeling. I was aching and ACHING with unhappiness. With confusion.

About Bill. About the walls. About *everything*.

Because everything was wrong, everything was messed up—and I had no idea how to make things right.

Just one thing I *did* know. One thing only.

Wallboggling was a useless USELESS skill. No good for anything. NOTHING AT ALL.

**26**

Isabel was hard at work next morning. I went downstairs, and there she was, standing at her easel. She had her painting smock on, a big frown on her face, a splodgy green cheek, and a drooping mouth.

She looked small and sad, as she put one last dab of paint on a big splatty mess—swirls of greens and browns with one red splodge.

'That's a good painting,' I said.

Because I had decided—maybe I *did* have power. Power over how I dealt with all the changes. And maybe it was time to make some changes of my own. Starting right now, right here, at home.

Isabel's mouth drooped even more. 'It is a SAD painting,' she said, in a mournful sort of whisper. 'Its name is "Dead Ladybird Under Leaves in the Moonlight".'

She pointed her finger. 'The mummy ladybird is died,' she whispered. 'She is died under the leaves.

And she is died from SADNESS. Because the ladybird babies is all died too. Gobbled up by an owl.'

Oh dear. Isabel was really NOT happy.

'What about that one?' I said, pointing at another painting, drying on the kitchen table. Mainly red and blue with black blobs.

'That is an EVEN MORE SAD painting,' she whispered, mouth drooping more. 'And scary. Its name is "Night Things Creeping in the Bedroom".'

She pointed to two blue blobs in one corner. 'That is my eyes,' she said. 'Peeking out from under my duvet. And Moo-Moo and Flufferty are in the painting, but hiding COMPLETELY under my duvet, with their eyes tight shut.'

Then her shoulders slumped. 'Want to go home,' she said.

'This *is* home,' I said.

'Not,' said Isabel. 'Home is where Mummy is.'

Then Dad came into the room, and Isabel's mouth started wobbling. She drooped past Dad. 'I am going to look after Moo-Moo and Flufferty,' she whispered to him. 'Because they are VERY sad.'

Dad sat down at the table, and ran his hands through his hair. 'What do I do?' he said. 'Ned, what do I do?'

I thought about it. 'Stickers,' I said. 'A sticker chart. Isabel LOVES stickers.'

So me and Dad made a chart. Ten columns, ten rows. One hundred squares, just the right size for stickers. Then I got some stickers that had been sitting in my drawer since Christmas. And added a title to the chart...

## ISABEL'S STICKER CHART

She spotted it straight off. Soon as she came back into the kitchen, clutching Moo-Moo and Flufferty.

She gasped. 'A sticker chart!' she said. And a smile lit up her whole face.

I was ready. I held out the stickers. 'Smiling nicely,' I said. 'That is worth a sticker. Definitely!'

Then I let Isabel choose one to stick on the chart.

By the end of breakfast Isabel had another three stickers. For eating all her toast, for telling Daddy he was as good as Mummy at butter spreading, and for carrying her plate to the sink.

Which just left Grace to sort out...

I knew Grace was in her room. She'd been there ever since she came back yesterday.

I stood outside the door and listened. I could hear sniffing coming from inside, lots of sniffing. So I knocked.

'Go away!' Grace yelled. But I ignored her, and went in.

Grace was lying face-down on her bed. She turned over and sat up when she saw me. She had red eyes, a red nose, and messed-up hair.

'He dumped me,' she hissed, sniffing more. 'You were right. He *has* gone off me. It's over. Me and George are history. Happy now?'

I stood there, wondering what to do.

Because sometimes, I find, Grace asks questions that she doesn't actually want answering. So—was this one of those? Or the other sort? The sort she actually *does* want answering?

But, if so, what should my answer be? That, yes, I was happy she was rid of him, because he was an idiot? Was that the right thing to say? I wasn't sure.

In the end, I said this...

'No,' I said. 'I'm not happy. Not if you're sad.'

Then I waited. Was that OK?

It seemed to be. Because Grace gave one more sniff, then started hissing again. 'All summer,' she hissed, 'all the time we were away, all the messages—about how much he was missing me... *Lies.*'

Now Grace paused. 'Because,' she hissed, 'he was NOT missing me. He was too busy two-timing me *all* summer! With TARIKA!'

*Woah.*

This was teenage stuff. WAY over my head.

George... he was seeing Tarika, at the same time as seeing Grace... And Tarika... she was one of Grace's best friends...

At least, she used to be.

So I panicked. What to do? How could I help?

Then Grace spoke again. 'And now I've been back a whole week he's decided he prefers Tarika,' she hissed.

Just then, her phone beeped. A text.

Grace read it. She flung her phone on the bed. 'It's from Mel,' she hissed. 'She says she doesn't want me to feel more upset and worthless than she's sure I *already* feel because of being dumped. But, as a true friend, she wants me to know that George is using the voucher I bought him for his birthday to take Tarika for food at Brunchies—right this minute.'

Then—oh no—Grace threw back her head, and she started to howl. Shrieking howls, like a horribly injured wild animal.

I panicked more.

I had to stop the howling. I had to *do* something. But what? What could I do?

Then I realized what I could do...

So I did it.

I boggled straight out through Grace's bedroom wall.

That did the trick. The howling stopped—straight away.

So I boggled back through the wall.

Grace was sitting there, eyes wide. 'Wow,' she said. 'WOW...'

I held up my hand. 'Oops, forgot something,' I said. 'Won't be long.'

Then I whizzed out through the wall again and into my room. Collected some things, whizzed back, then put the things down on Grace's bed.

She stared...

Itching Powder!
It's scratch-tastic!

Smelly slime!
A thousand uses!

'George will be out of his house this morning,' I said to Grace. 'And I can walk through walls.'

Then I pointed at the itching powder. 'Shame if this ended up in his bedding,' I said, shaking my head sadly. 'He'd probably have a horribly itchy night.'

Then I pointed again, at the smelly slime. 'Even *more* of a shame if some of this found its way into his socks,' I said, still shaking my head sadly. 'And his football boots.'

Grace gaped at me. Then a big grin spread across her face. She leapt to her feet.

Then my sister—my teenage sister—lifted me up, and twirled me round. And gave me a big smacking kiss on the cheek.

'Let's go!' she said.

**27**

A good deed! I did a good deed for Grace with my wallboggling!

Because me and Grace rushed off to George's house. No one was in, not George, or his mum, or his dad—so Grace found me a good bit of wall to boggle through. A kitchen wall, one with no cupboards on it.

She forgot about the dog though...

Donald. Small and yappy. A bundle of bristling orange fur that hurled himself straight at me as I boggled into the kitchen.

I dodged round Donald—just. Then shot out of the kitchen, and slammed the door shut...

Donald stood by the kitchen door, and yapped. He yapped and yapped, the whole time I was up in George's bedroom, carefully distributing all the itching powder and slime.

Donald was still yapping when I boggled my way out through the sitting room wall. And Grace could NOT stop grinning, all the way home. She grinned, she whooped, she slapped me on the back, grinned more. And we chatted. Not just about my wallboggling—although LOTS about that—but other stuff too. About the walls. About George. About Bill. And about Matilda Arkle...

Because that last time in the locked room, I'd read more of Matilda Arkle's Book of Secrets. Read something *intriguing*, on a page dated 2 July...

The STRANGEST of events occurred today—whilst I was embroidering a handkerchief, the most TEDIOUS of tasks.

I sat there, dreaming of escape. Dreaming of adventures.

'How is it that this schoolroom has a globe of the world, showing so many places, so full of excitement— yet all I learn is stitching and manners, and the correct way to curtsey?' I enquired of my governess.

That wretched old crone simply pursed her lips, and made no reply.

So I sat and I sizzled. 'I swear one day I shall BURST with boredom,' I announced.

Yet still that withered old hag stayed silent. So I leapt to my feet and I screamed.

'HELP ME!' I screamed, staggering and clutching

at my throat. 'Call for the DOCTOR! For I am the most unfortunate of children! I shall burst! I shall BURST! I shall actually EXPIRE with boredom!'

Then I flung myself to the floor and lay still, eyes staring, tongue lolling, in the manner of one who has departed this world...

The wretched creature LOCKED ME IN THE SCHOOLROOM.

'I shall leave you here for two hours,' she said, a gloat in her voice, and a gleam in her eye. 'And upon my return I shall find your initials embroidered on ALL THREE of these handkerchiefs.'

So I sat, alone, and I began to stitch. Sizzling and fizzling with anger. At this room, this prison, these four walls that entrapped me.

Anger so SIZZLINGLY, FIZZLINGLY strong—it sent my head spinning and spinning and spinning...

But then, dear Book—something happened. Something truly ASTONISHING!

I sat there, reading in the locked room, gripped. What happened? All that sizzling, fizzling anger... What happened?

So I turned the page, longing to know more.

Then I read this...

*I do not plan to TELL of what happened, dear Book. It is too IMPORTANT a secret to write in these pages. A SECRET SKILL that NO ONE must know of. The BEST, the MOST THRILLING of secrets I have EVER had!*

*All I shall say is this.*

*That my Book of Secrets is now at an end. For, with my most EXCELLENT of skills, I am simply TOO BUSY to write any more.*

*I bid you, dear Book, FAREWELL.*

That was it. The end of Matilda Arkle's Book of Secrets.

So I told Grace all about it—me boggling into the locked room, finding the Book of Secrets, reading the very last entry...

And Grace listened, goggle-eyed. 'Wow,' she said. 'Looks like Matilda Arkle was a wallboggler too. The first Arkle wallboggler!'

Then her eyes narrowed. 'Or maybe she got *another* magic skill. A DIFFERENT magic skill! Like teleporting!'

Now Grace's eyebrows were knotting. 'So... Matilda Arkle—she must have had a magic gene,' she said.

I gaped at Grace. 'A *magic* gene?' I said.

'Yes,' she said. 'And you inherited it.'

Then her eyes lit up. 'And maybe it's not just *you*

who got the magic gene. Maybe *I've* got it! Maybe I'll get a magic skill, or Isabel! And Matilda Arkle had lots of kids—FIVE, at *least*—and about TWENTY grandchildren! So there could be *other* kids out there, other Arkle descendants, getting magic skills!'

Could Grace be right? I had no idea. So I smiled at her, just happy we were chatting again. Because me and Grace used to chat much more, before all the new walls. And it felt good—so SO good—to be chatting again.

28

Back home, I packed up my garbage gobbler.

I made my garbage gobbler two years ago, out of papier mâché and paint. It's a bin—but not an ordinary sort of bin.

No.

The garbage gobbler is a crouching purple monster. It has a huge head, big bulging eyes, and a wide open mouth—the bin opening—with lots of jagged teeth. It's my most precious possession.

Bill loves it.

Bill is always screwing up bits of paper and aiming them into the mouth of my garbage gobbler.

Well now I was giving the garbage gobbler to Bill. I wanted to put things right. For Bill to be my friend again. A more equal friend, like he said.

Then, AT LAST, I could show him my wallboggling.

But halfway to Bill's I met the Clodd, sitting on a bench, clutching her phone and staring out to sea. And somehow—I'm not sure quite how—I ended up telling her my plan.

She listened, then looked at me. Did the eye-narrowing thing again.

'So… you think giving Bill your garbage gobbler will make him forget all the yelling, the bossing, the trap-setting? All that?' she said.

'No,' I said grumpily. 'I'm not THAT much of an idiot. I know I have to do some grovelling.'

The Clodd nodded. 'You do,' she said. '*Lots* of grovelling.'

'So… any grovelling tips?' I said, feeling even grumpier. Because I didn't want to ask the Clodd for grovelling advice—but I *did* want this to work.

So the Clodd ended up walking with me towards Bill's. Giving me grovelling tips on the way.

'First,' she said, 'Do some visual grovelling. LOOK like a groveller. No frowning, no scowling, wipe that grumpy look off your face—and look penitent.'

'Look penitent?' I said. 'OK…'

Then I started nodding, as if I knew what penitent meant. Which I didn't. But I was NOT admitting that to the Clodd.

There was no fooling her though. She worked it out

for herself, just by looking at me. It was scary. Like she was a mind reader.

'Penitent means looking sorry for being such an idiot,' the Clodd said. 'You have to look really sorry—'

'I *am* really sorry,' I said.

'So SHOW him,' said the Clodd. 'Let Bill see your grovelling. Cast your eyes down. Scuff your feet. Like this.'

The Clodd stood there, hanging her head, mouth turned down, shoulders slumped—looking utterly miserable and ashamed of herself.

Then she looked up, and snapped back to normal. 'Second,' she said, 'do some verbal grovelling.'

'Verbal grovelling?' I said.

'TELL Bill you're sorry,' she said. 'Tell him you know what an idiot you've been. Tell him you wouldn't blame him for never wanting to be the friend of an idiot. And tell him you are planning to be LESS of an idiot in future.'

Then she jabbed me with her finger. 'But be *truthful* in your grovelling,' she said. 'Speak from your heart. If you really want him to be your friend, you've got to MEAN the grovelling.'

'I do mean it,' I said. 'I *do* think I've been a bad friend.'

Now the Clodd's finger stopped jabbing and started wagging, right in my face.

'But do NOT promise things in your grovelling that you can't deliver,' she said. 'Don't promise Bill you'll never be an idiot again—because chances are you *will* be. You can't change overnight. So promise you'll try your VERY hardest not to be an idiot, but that, if you are accidentally being one, he is to tell you.'

I felt a bit dazed. Grovelling seemed extremely complicated.

And there was more.

'Third,' said the Clodd, 'LISTEN. A good groveller does lots of listening. When Bill speaks, do NOT butt in. Let him talk. Just listen. And think—HARD—about what he's saying.'

My head was spinning. 'So... let me check I've got this right,' I said. 'I have to *look* sorry for being an idiot. *Say* sorry for being an idiot. And *listen* when Bill tells me that, yes, I have been an idiot.'

The Clodd nodded. 'You do all that,' she said, 'and the grovelling *might* work.'

Then she peered right at me. 'You're quaking,' she said. 'Like you did at the custard.'

I wasn't surprised. I felt terrified.

'It's just...' I mumbled. 'I haven't done much grovelling. I'm only a beginner at grovelling. Suppose I don't grovel well enough?'

'At least you'll have tried,' the Clodd said.

Then she looked thoughtful again. 'It is possible the grovelling might not have an IMMEDIATE effect,' she said. 'That Bill will need time to think about your grovelling, then get back to you. But—'

She shrieked.

A shape had just shot out from behind the brick shelter, right beside us.

Snapper.

He grabbed the Clodd's phone—and charged off to his bike, which was lying on the ground. He leapt on, got pedalling, and disappeared down the footpath.

I was shocked. Truly shocked. I did NOT expect that. Stealing Swizzlers was one thing—but a phone...What was *wrong* with Snapper?

The Clodd had big tears in her eyes—not sad tears. Tears of RAGE.

'That phone,' she hissed, 'it's my most PRECIOUS thing. My way of keeping in touch with Ruby. And I *have* to get it back.'

'We should tell a grown-up,' I said. 'Report it.'

The Clodd ignored me. She grabbed my arm. 'We can't prove he took it,' she said. 'I'll have to get it back myself. Ruby could be ringing any time.'

The Clodd started nodding her head up and down. 'That's it,' she said, a determined look on her pointy face. 'I'm going to get it back. So—where does he live?'

'Where does he *live*?' I said. 'What are you planning on doing? Knocking on the front door, and asking him nicely to give your phone back?'

The Clodd shook her head. 'Course not,' she said, rolling her eyes. 'I'm breaking in. Somehow. And first, I need to case the joint.'

I felt my heart sink. This was NOT part of my plan. I wanted to go and see Bill. Give him the garbage gobbler. Let him be the first kid in class to see my wallboggling.

But I realized. My plan had to change.

Because the Clodd—whatever I said—was NOT going to listen. She was going to try and break in to get that phone back. And Snapper would catch her doing it. He'd be bound to.

So—even though I did NOT want to do it—I *had* to . . .

'There IS a way to get it back,' I said. 'Watch this.'

And that's when I walked through the wall of the shelter. And back again.

The Clodd let out a shriek. A piercing shriek. An utterly astonished shriek.

She started swaying about, her mouth opening and shutting like a goldfish.

'Yo… I… wa… nnnn dddd?' she stuttered, pointing at the shelter wall, then at me. 'Ha… wh… wa… yyy… dddd?'

Then she took a deep breath and tried again. 'Dd…' she said, still stuttering, and grabbing me by my hoodie. 'Dddd… yyy?'

More big breaths, more trying. Then, she got there.

'How did you DO that?' she said. 'How? How? HOW?'

I shrugged. 'Dunno,' I said. 'I just can. I call it wallboggling.'

That was *not* good enough for the Clodd. She started rattling off questions, right in my face. One after another they came out—*rat-tat-tat*—like a machine gun.

'Do *all* your family do wallboggling?' she demanded. 'ALL of them? Are your family magicians? REAL magicians? Can anyone learn to do wallboggling? Can *I* learn to do it? Is it like learning juggling, or tightrope walking? But… *when* did it happen? *How* did it happen? Have you ALWAYS been able to do it? Did you just wake up one day, a wallboggler? Can you do other stuff, not just wallboggling? And if you can—what other stuff? Does wallboggling hurt? Does it feel weird? How do you keep wallboggling SECRET?'

Then, exhausted, she slumped against the wall of the shelter.

'You finished?' I said.

She nodded. 'Think so,' she said, very faintly.

'Then let's go,' I said. 'We've got a phone to get back.'

29

I got kitted out back at the Clodd's. Because she had the *Secret Sleuth* kit. Not the basic *Secret Sleuth* kit, like I had—but the *deluxe* version. The version I was saving up for. The one I had dreams about owning.

She opened the box, and it had everything. Everything a kid could need to go sleuthing.

Disguises—lots of disguises. Not just a false moustache and one wig, which my kit had. But lots of wigs, and glasses, and stick-on freckles and warts. A box of quality face paints, with instructions for doing scars and wounds. And hats, including a balaclava—which the Clodd handed to me.

The kit had all sorts of equipment too. Binoculars, a microscope and slides for examining evidence, a polaroid camera for scene-of-the-crime pictures, dusting powder for fingerprints, plaster of Paris for making casts, a magnifying glass, scissors, tweezers, a notebook, an invisible ink pen, a shiny silver head torch…

The Clodd handed me the head torch. 'Might have to search dark cupboards,' she said. Then she took out one last thing. Small and round and flat, with one jagged edge...

I recognized it from the basic kit. A bird whistle—a useless bird whistle.

Because I had followed all the instructions when I got *my* kit. I'd clamped it in my mouth, just like the diagram showed, leaving air around it. I'd blown and made a 'ch' sort of sound, like I was about to say 'challenge' or 'chuckle'. Then I'd moved it with my lips and my tongue, and tried to talk like normal. That was supposed to make what came out of the whistle sound like a bird noise.

But it didn't.

I could NOT make the whistle work.

'I'll take this,' said the Clodd, plucking her whistle from the kit. Then she stuck it in her mouth—and out came this astonishing noise. Like the trills of a bird. A real bird... not a kid pretending to be one.

I was impressed, but also fed up. How come the Clodd could make it work when I couldn't? So I started scowling at her again. Then I stopped.

I had a feeling that scowling could be wrong. The sort of thing an idiot did. And if I wanted to be Bill's friend again, maybe I should get some practice in on the Clodd.

So…

'Not bad,' I said, but it was hard. SO hard. It felt like the words were strangling me as I spoke them.

The Clodd stared at me. 'Hm,' she said, looking thoughtful, eyes narrowed.

Then she started nodding. 'I get it,' she said. 'You can't make the whistle work, can you?'

'Course I can,' I said.

She rolled her eyes. 'Whatever,' she said. 'The whistle is the signal. And if you hear it—get out. Fast!'

Snapper's house has hedges all round it, and the cliffs at the back. I crouched behind a side hedge, and stared.

I used to go to Snapper's house a lot, back when we were friends—but it was different now. Bigger. It had been added to—almost doubled in size. A big house now, for just Snapper and his dad.

I gulped.

It was one thing having a plan. Another thing actually *doing* it. Actually boggling into his house, and finding his room.

Right now, there was no sign of Snapper. But his bike was in the front garden, propped up by a big shed with a half-open door, so he must have come home. Was he still here? And what about the dad? How could I know if the house was empty?

I couldn't.

So—suppose I got *caught* wallboggling. What then? Could a boy be sent to PRISON for wallboggling?

'Which one's his room?' the Clodd whispered, looking up at the first floor. 'Which window?'

'How would *I* know?' I hissed at her. 'The house is all different, and it's wallboggling I do, not X-ray vision.'

I couldn't help hissing. I was terrified. Now we were here, the plan seemed risky. VERY risky.

The Clodd ignored the hissing and went creeping along the hedge, looking up at the windows. I followed her round the back of the house.

Then the Clodd stopped.

So did I.

We both stared up at a window. A window with a mask dangling down. A gruesome mask. A big ugly head—one bulging eyeball, lots of scars, huge teeth like fangs, and trails of red blood dripping down its chin.

That was Snapper's room. It had to be.

So I pulled the balaclava right down over my face. It was time for some wallboggling.

\* \* \*

My teeth were clacking, my knees were knocking—but I made it through the wall and into Snapper's kitchen, all gleaming and brand-new.

I tiptoed out into the hallway. It had a huge mirror, almost the length of the wall, with a lot of the sitting room reflected in it.

No one was in there.

I listened. No sounds of anyone in the house. No TV. No music. No games.

So, on trembling legs, I headed for the stairs. I tiptoed up them, past the bathroom, and along the corridor.

I stopped by the first open door. Yes, this was it. Snapper's bedroom. Smelly, a bit messy, full of old socks and mugs with mouldy stuff in them, the mask dangling in the window.

And there, right on the desk—was the Clodd's phone...

I snatched up the phone, but then I heard two things. The slam of a shed door... And the whistle...

The bird whistle, the warning. Louder and louder.

Snapper—or someone—must have been in the shed. And now the front door was opening, then banging shut.

I heard footsteps. Fast footsteps, coming towards the stairs. Up the stairs...

I panicked. I was *trapped.* What could I do? Where could I go? Not out through Snapper's bedroom door. I'd be spotted on the landing.

So I did the only thing I could think of. I boggled through the bedroom wall, and into the bathroom...

Just as the bathroom door was flung open—and in walked Snapper.

**30**

I froze to the spot, and so did Snapper. He looked *dazed*. Staring at me, balaclava pulled over my face— just my eyes and mouth poking out... At the wall I had just boggled through... At me again... At the wall again...

He took a step nearer, peering hard, eyes narrowed, 'Ned?' he said, uncertainly. '*Ned?* Is that you?'

Then he spotted Maddie's phone clutched in my hand, and a flush crept across his face. A guilty flush.

Guilty? Snapper looking *guilty?* I did NOT expect that.

Then, once more, the front door opened. It shut with a slam, and a voice called out. A mean voice. A taunting voice. A voice I'd heard somewhere before...

'Sammy, oh Sammy Boy... Where ARE you?'

Snapper's face got a hunted sort of look. His head swivelled sideways, towards the stairs, then back towards me.

He took a step forward. Then a step back. And I could see—he had no idea what to do. Deal with the wallboggler upstairs, or the voice downstairs.

'*Waiting*, Sammy!' the voice called out, all singsong and gloating. 'Waiting for YOOOOU!'

Snapper's head swivelled again. Then he decided. He put a finger to his lips and scurried towards the stairs.

My head was spinning. That finger, Snapper's finger—it was a *warning* finger. *Keep quiet*, the finger was saying.

What was going on?

I tiptoed along the landing, then crouched at the top of the stairs, part-hidden by a table and a big yellow jug with blue flowers painted all over it.

I peeked down. And there, reflected in the hallway mirror, lounging in an armchair in the sitting room— was the Hulk.

But... what was the Hulk doing *here*? And why was he smiling at Snapper that way? The way a shark smiles at a sardine?

Now the Hulk clicked his fingers. 'Laces,' he said, pointing down at his trainers. 'Undo them.'

I felt my mouth drop open.

Snapper was standing there, not moving. Then his

head started shaking. 'No more,' he said—and it was a shock to hear Snapper's voice, all tiny and trembling. 'No more.'

The Hulk just stared at him. 'You broke my phone,' he said. 'Where's the replacement you promised?'

So *that* was it—the reason why Snapper stole Maddie's phone. To give to the Hulk.

But Snapper was still shaking his head. 'It was an accident. You made me jump and that's what made me knock the phone off the counter. And if you hadn't hidden behind the door, pretending to be the Craggelton poltergeist, then hurled that pan across the kitchen—I *wouldn't* have jumped. So, actually, it's mainly your fault.'

Now Snapper's voice trembled more and more. 'And all this...' he said, pointing at the Hulk's shoes. 'Stop. Just stop.'

The Hulk smirked. 'I don't *want* to stop,' he said.

Then he leant forward—the smirk gone, a big scowl on his face. 'And another thing I don't want,' he said, 'is to live with a stupid little STEPBROTHER.'

Stepbrother? The Hulk was Snapper's *stepbrother*?

The Hulk leant back and folded his arms. 'I was happy living with just my mum,' he said. 'I NEVER wanted to move here.'

Now I understood. Seeing the Hulk around these last few months—that must be when he moved here. When Snapper got worse...

So all those twitching, shifty looks, all the punches—they were all because Snapper was miserable. Scared and miserable... bullied by his stepbrother.

And, as I stood there, the impossible was happening. I was feeling SORRY for Snapper.

'I was happy living with just my dad,' said Snapper, still all trembly. 'And I never wanted you to move here either. But kids don't get to choose.'

Now the Hulk had an evil smirk on his face. 'Oh, kids do get to choose,' he said. 'Or rather...YOU do.'

Then he held up two bits of seaweed—one long and thin, all in strands, and one fat, with bobbly bits

'They're mine,' said Snapper, making a lunge for them. 'My samples. I was drying them out... to study.'

'They're mine now, my little marine biologist,' said the Hulk, whipping them out of Snapper's reach Then he stood up, towering over Snapper—and a big sly grin stretched itself right across his face.

'And you,' he said, 'are eating one of them.' He paused. 'But I'll let you choose which.'

I was shocked. Totally shocked.

No. No. *No*. That was a truly FIENDISH plan. A kid should *not* be made to eat seaweed.

So I leapt to my feet, and knocked the big flowery jug straight off the table with my elbow.

Down the jug went, bouncing noisily from step to step. Then it smashed to pieces on the hallway floor.

Straight away, I heard feet. Two sets of feet, one light, one heavy, pounding across the sitting room. Then, a bellowing voice.

'Who's there?' the Hulk bellowed, hurtling towards the hallway. 'Who's up there? Whoever you are, I'll FIND you!'

I shot off the landing and into the bathroom. I knew what I had to do—keep one boggle ahead of the Hulk at ALL times.

'Give yourself up!' the Hulk shouted, pounding up the stairs. 'Whoever you are, give yourself up!'

I boggled into Snapper's bedroom then rushed towards the far wall—knocking into things, sending things flying off the desk and across the floor as I ran.

'I hear you!' yelled the Hulk. 'I know where you are! You're TRAPPED!' And now those feet came pounding towards Snapper's bedroom—just as I boggled out through the far wall.

'I know you're in here somewhere,' he bellowed, charging into Snapper's room. 'And there's two of us but only one of you!'

I could hear cupboards being hurled open. Things being dragged, things being moved. And lots of scuffling noises, checking noises. Checking—by the sound of it—in every corner.

Then the sounds stopped. 'Where is he?' said the Hulk, sounding baffled.

'He's not in here,' said another voice. Snapper's, less trembly now. 'There's nowhere else to hide.'

'He *has* to be in here, idiot!' the Hulk spat. 'We'd have spotted him on the landing. There's no other way out.'

He paused, then had another idea. 'Unless...' he said, 'the window—maybe he got out of the window. Unlocked it.'

I could hear him march across to the window. But...

'It's locked,' he muttered, and his voice didn't sound quite so tough now. 'The window is *locked*.'

Another pause...

'But... he was definitely in here. All my stuff's been knocked about. And the jug on the landing... things don't just fall by *themselves*.'

All *his* stuff... So not Snapper's bedroom then, but the Hulk's. And now, come to think of it, this room—the one I was tiptoeing across—must be Snapper's. No doubt about it.

It had a shelf full of books about oceans. Flippers and a snorkel on the bed. A microscope on the desk. And a lobster pot on the floor—which I had just tripped over.

Smash! The lobster pot broke into pieces and I tottered backwards, setting off Snapper's jellyfish wind chimes, which were dangling in the window.

And here they came again—those pounding feet, out on to the landing. Fast as I could, I boggled once more, back into the Hulk's bedroom.

I listened. More checking, more searching. Then...

'There's no one here,' the Hulk said. 'NO ONE.' And now his voice dropped to almost a whisper...

'Is it *here*? The Craggelton poltergeist... Is it HERE?'

And the words of the Clodd popped into my head...

'*Even the biggest toughest kids are scared of SOMETHING.*'

Now the Hulk started whimpering. 'Poltergeist,' he called, shakily. 'Wherever you are—*listen* to me! I'll be the BEST stepbrother in the world! I'll help Sam with his homework. Fractions, I'm brilliant at fractions. I'll help him with ALL his fractions. Just leave me alone! Leave this place!'

I thought hard.

Snapper—he used to be my friend, though he wasn't any more.

BUT...

He was having trouble. A *lot* of trouble with his stepbrother, the Hulk. And that had to STOP.

So I knocked—hard—on the wall. One knock, two knocks, three...

The Hulk yelped. 'Knocking noises!' he shrieked. 'Knocking noises!'

Then I heard his feet pounding along the landing, down the stairs, and out through the front door.

**31**

I heard more feet. Snapper's. He came and stood in the doorway.

I pulled the balaclava off, and glared. I did NOT want to speak to Snapper. I didn't want the Hulk bullying him—but I didn't want to be his friend either. Too many years. Too many pranks. Too many shoves.

But Snapper stood there, head hanging down. 'Ned,' he mumbled. 'All those knocking noises... Thanks.'

I didn't say a word. I had nothing to say. I could see he was *itching* to ask me about the wallboggling—but not daring. And I was NOT planning on helping him out. So I just watched him, standing there, shuffling from foot to foot, looking awkward.

'And all the stuff I did to you...' Snapper mumbled now. 'Sorry.'

I looked him in the eyes. 'No more kicking, then,' I said. 'No more punching. No more anything.'

Snapper nodded. 'No more,' he said.

'That goes for Bill too,' I said.

Snapper nodded again.

'Good,' I said. 'I'll go and tell him.'

'I saw him,' Snapper said. 'Just now, from the window. Looked like he was heading for the beach.'

I nodded. Then turned and walked straight for the stairs.

I boggled out through the kitchen wall. But that wallboggle... did it feel slower? More effort? It was hard to tell. Maybe it was just a very thick wall.

The Clodd leapt on me as soon as I came round the side of the hedge.

'Information,' she said, grabbing my arm. 'I need INFORMATION. What *happened* in there? What? WHAT?'

'First things first,' I said. Then I handed her the phone.

The Clodd clutched at it like it was the most precious jewel in the world. She switched it on, then showed me a picture.

A little kid. A mini-Clodd. Corkscrew curls, conker eyes—and dressed as a witch. With her hands stretched out like claws.

'Ruby,' she said.

She nodded at the head torch sticking out of my

pocket. 'That's yours, by the way,' she said. 'If you want it.'

Which, I think, was the Clodd's way of thanking me.

I gave the Clodd a quick update on all the boggling. And she listened, eyes gleaming, head nodding.

'Nice work,' she said. 'Not such an idiot after all.'

Then she paused, scrabbled under the hedge and pulled out my backpack, garbage gobbler stuffed inside. 'Let's hope Bill thinks the same,' she said, handing it to me.

It was windier now, and big grey storm clouds were billowing in from the sea, whipping up the waves, as I ran towards the beach.

I had the Clodd's last words of advice going through my head.

'Remember,' she told me, as she set off for home. 'Look sorry, say sorry, and do NOT butt in when Bill speaks.'

The tide was coming in fast now, waves crashing over the rocks. And the beach was almost deserted— just a couple of dog walkers.

But no sign of Bill.

I stared right and left as the first drops of rain

spattered down on to my head. Then I spotted him. At the far end of the beach, clambering up the rocks.

Where was he going? To the caves?

I checked my watch. He had time—but not lots of it. Soon the sea would be swirling up the rocks, towards the caves.

I ran across the beach. Scrambled up the rocks, fast as I could. And there was Bill—already by the cave entrance, stooping to pick up a sharp bit of rock.

I scrambled down. 'Bill!' I shouted. 'Bill!' Then I jumped off the rocks and ran towards him.

Bill turned to face me with a BIG scowl on his face. He was *not* happy to see me, not at all.

I skidded over to him. Then I took a deep breath. 'Bill,' I said. 'I am sorry—TRULY sorry—for being an idiot.'

Bill scowled more, his chin jutting right out. And said nothing. Not a *word*.

I gulped. That was some scowl on Bill's face. 'I've done lots of things wrong,' I said. 'I know I have. And I have NOT been a true friend. Not to you. Not at all.'

Then I opened my backpack.

'I can't actually EXPLAIN how sorry I am,' I said. 'But I can SHOW you. So—this is for you. It's yours to keep. For ever.'

And out it came. My garbage gobbler—big bulging eyes, wide open mouth. My most *precious* possession.

Bill stared at it. Then, slowly, he reached out his hands and took it.

I held my breath.

Would it work? Would the garbage gobbler make everything *right*?

No.

Because Bill put the garbage gobbler down on the ground—and started jumping all over it.

Up and down, up and down he jumped. Again and again.

I stood there, shocked. My garbage gobbler was DESTROYED. Crushed to pieces.

And Bill was standing there, arms folded, an even *bigger* scowl on his face.

I stared down. Stared and stared at the crumpled remains of my garbage gobbler—and I felt all crumpled inside.

This was worse than Bill exploding at me. Much worse. How angry must Bill be with me to do *THAT*?

Was I *that* bad?

A tiny bit of my insides *un*crumpled. I started to feel indignant. No. I was NOT that bad. I *wasn't*.

But Bill thought I was. Because now he stuck his nose in the air and turned away.

No, no, NO. This had to stop! Because I could see— Bill was determined NOT to be my friend.

Well—I was determined he *would* be. So it was time to try one last thing. And this *had* to work.

'Bill, listen!' I said, urgently. 'Give me ONE LAST CHANCE! The secret… the Tower Two secret—I'll show you! Right now! Because something happened to me five days ago. I got… well, a *skill*.'

Bill had his back to me now. He was kicking the cave wall. Arms still folded.

'You have to turn *around*,' I said. 'You have to *watch* me, *see* the secret skill. And I promise—you will NOT believe your eyes.'

I could see Bill struggling. Not wanting to turn around, but wanting to, both at the same time.

Then Bill did turn. VERY slowly.

He gave me the biggest scowl he could. And spoke, through gritted teeth. 'This,' he hissed, 'had better be *good*!'

'It is,' I said. 'Oh it is.'

Then I took a deep breath—and boggled my way into the cave, through the wall…

\* \* \*

I stood inside the cave, waiting, as Bill came hurtling in.

I could see straight off—my wallboggling had NOT made things better. It had made things *worse*.

Bill was SNARLING with rage. Spluttering. Gnashing his teeth. He could hardly speak he was so full of fury.

'That!' he hissed. '*That?* You kept that secret for FIVE WHOLE DAYS? A magic skill? And you never told me? I will NEVER forgive you! NEVER!'

Now that was not FAIR. I started to feel even more indignant. 'I did *try* to tell you,' I said. 'I—'

But Bill wasn't listening. He was too busy grabbing me by the T-shirt.

'Do you know why I came here?' he hissed. 'To scratch that *stupid* Tower Two message OFF the wall!'

Then he gave me a big push, then another, and another—until he'd pushed me right out of the cave.

'Go, go, GO!' he hissed. 'Because you and me—we will never be friends. Not EVER again!'

## 32

I stomped off, hurt, indignant feelings swirling around inside me. *Furious* feelings.

The wallboggling—Bill was NOT being fair about it. All the snarling at me, all the hissing for keeping my wallboggling secret.

I wasn't *trying* to keep it secret. I didn't *want* to keep it secret. I would have shown Bill my wallboggling straight away. It was HIS fault I didn't.

His fault for being busy with Lekeisha. Busy with Harriet and Errol. Busy being off sick. There were lots of times I would have shown him my wallboggling, but I couldn't.

And now—I *had* shown him. But instead of being impressed, he just gnashed his teeth and pushed me. Pushed me right out of the cave.

That was not fair either. Bill should NOT have behaved like that.

And as for jumping on my garbage gobbler... that

was MEAN. Because, yes, I had done a LOT of things wrong, but I was trying to make up for it. I was trying to put things right. But Bill was *refusing* to let me.

So I stomped across the sand—what little was left of it—and started climbing the rocks.

I could picture Bill right now. He'd be crouched down, that scowl across his face. Scratching at the Tower Two message. Getting rid of every trace of it.

Muttering, probably. Muttering—angrily—about me keeping my wallboggling secret. Muttering about me being the worst friend in the world.

Well, maybe I was. Maybe I *had* been. But Bill had had a chance to forgive me, a chance to put things behind us, to start again. And he had FAILED to take it.

Well, good RIDDANCE. I was better off without him.

I *was*.

Well—I tried to make myself think that. But I didn't, not really. Not at all.

I plonked myself down at the top of the rocks. Stared at the sea, a lot nearer now. The waves bigger, closer. Moving fast over the rocks.

I could smell the salt spray in the air, hear the cries— all mournful and echoing—of the gulls circling over the cliffs. And, as I sat there, more and more feelings washed through me.

SAD feelings. Lonely, regretful feelings. Because more than anything, I wanted one thing. For me and Bill to be friends again.

I thought back over the last year. Remembering all the fun me and Bill had had, down here on the beach— building sand robots, checking rock pools, exploring the caves.

Remembering our Tower Two meetings, all the secret stuff. And the day I'd told Bill my secret fear, of custard. And he'd told me his, of eating a spider in his sleep.We swore to keep each other's secret fear safe— and that was the day I realized Bill was the best friend I'd ever had.

But now he wasn't.

I'd tried, really tried. Said I was sorry. Given him my garbage gobbler. None of it had worked. Even showing him my wallboggling hadn't made us friends again.

And, ringing loud in my ears, I could hear the last words Bill had said.

*You and me—we will never be friends. Not EVER again!*

Not ever…

My friendship with Bill—it was over.

I ached. So full of miserable feelings, I was aching— inside, outside, all over me. Aching and aching.

Aching about Bill, *so* much about Bill… But something else too.

Aching about wallboggling. Because being a wallboggler was no fun without Bill to share it with.

And another thing. Boggling through that cave wall, showing Bill my wallboggling—it felt harder to do. Definitely harder. It could have been because the cave wall was so thick. But it could have been something else…

My wallboggling could be slowing down. Running out. Maybe even *ending*.

Then, with a chill, I remembered my list—my wallboggling list. And question number six…

### Could I get STUCK while wallboggling?

I shivered. What a horrible *horrible* thought.

I had no idea how wallboggling worked, or how I did it. Maybe I *disappeared* while I was in the wall somehow, then reappeared as I came out.

So, if I got stuck—would I disappear FOR EVER?

Or, suppose I got stuck on the way *out* of the wall, half in, half out? What would happen then?

The fire brigade would have to cut ROUND me. Maybe I'd spend the rest of my life as part-boy, part-wall. Gawped at wherever I went.

But, if my wallboggling was getting harder … *why*?

Was it me being less angry about walls?

Because it was anger, furious anger with the walls, that seemed to—somehow—start it all off. Maybe I just wasn't angry enough, not now, not any more. Not with walls.

I thought back. Remembering that night, the night I first wallboggled.

The anger, the FURY with walls. Standing there, pummelling and kicking at that wall. And then—that whooshing feeling. The astonishment, the excitement as my fists, my foot, and then the rest of me went straight through that wall.

One minute an ordinary kid. The next—a wallboggler.

A wallboggler …

Five days I had been a wallboggler—was it really only five days—and what had I done?

Nothing much.

Nothing big. Nothing daring. Nothing good, like wallboggling into a burning building, and snatching a baby from the flames with only SECONDS to spare.

I stood up, ready to go.

I took one last look back. Where was Bill? He needed to leave the caves—and soon. The waves were speeding up the rocks now. Closer, much closer.

Then I heard something. A sound, over the noise of the wind and the waves. A cracking slithering sound. A *terrifying* sound...

And loud. So *so* LOUD.

**33**

That sound, that terrifying sound—it was coming from somewhere above me.

So I looked up. And I *froze*.

A whole chunk of the cliff was falling away. A vast chunk. The biggest rockfall I had EVER seen. Chunks of cliff, and stones and rocks and boulders...

All tumbling and tumbling, down and down. Then landing, piling up in a huge lumpy heap...

Right in front of the entrance to the caves.

No. NO!

The cave entrance—it was blocked. COMPLETELY blocked.

But Bill... *Bill!* He was still *inside!*

I scrambled back over the rocks, fast as I could. I hurled myself across the tiny strip of sand still left— then crouched down by the huge heap of rocks. 'Bill! BILL!' I yelled. 'Can you hear me?'

Silence.

I stood up, panicking. What to do?

Those lumps of rock—no way could I move them. No one could. This needed machines. Big machines. Like diggers.

But... a digger couldn't get here. Not now. Not in time. The sea was SO MUCH nearer. Sweeping over the rocks, faster and faster...

I had to leave. I HAD to. Before I got cut off—stranded here, up against the cliffs.

But I *couldn't* leave. I could NOT leave Bill.

'Bill!' I yelled again. 'Bill! SAY something!'

Silence.

But... *why*? Why the silence?

Bill wouldn't be giving me the silent treatment. Not *now*. And surely he could hear me—even with the rockfall? There were cracks. Spaces. Gaps. Big enough for sound to get through.

And then—shivers went through me, terrified shivers. Shivers from head to toe. Because those spaces, those gaps—it was not just sound that could get through...

It was SEA.

Yes. The sea could get in. Soon water would be swirling through those gaps, and into the caves...

'Bill' I yelled. '*Bill!*'

But there was STILL no answer.

Maybe Bill was *hurt*. Was that it?

Yes. That must be it. Bill was in there, but hurt—maybe *unconscious*. With the sea getting nearer and nearer. And only one person here to help him.

ME.

There was no choice. No choice AT ALL.

Bill was hurt, and he needed my help. So I *had* to do it. Had to boggle my way back into the cave, drag Bill to the cave wall, and boggle us both out. Then drag him over the rocks to safety.

Yes, that's what I had to do. And I had to do it FAST.

But...

Thoughts were rushing through my brain. Thoughts I did NOT want to think. Because this wall—it had been so hard, so slow to boggle through last time. And now, I had to do it *again*.

So suppose, this time, it was even *harder*? Suppose, this time, it was even *slower*? Suppose, this time—

No.

I crushed the thoughts down. Those thoughts had to GO. I was doing this. I *was*. Right now.

So I stood, and I stared. Stared and stared at the cave wall. Focused, then took a step forward...

It was difficult. So *SO* difficult. Like being in some terrifying nightmare.

My boggling had slowed right down. I was inside the wall—and the thing I had feared, the thing I had dreaded... It was coming true.

I was STUCK. Completely stuck in the wall.

I struggled. Panicked. I couldn't go back, couldn't go forward, couldn't move. But I had to move. *Had* to.

I struggled more. Panicked more. It felt as if the wall was trying to grab me. Trying to squash me, to squeeze me right into it. To swallow me up, until I was PART of it.

And there was pressure, so much pressure. Cold stone, all around me—so much pressure it HURT.

Then, with one final effort, one HUGE final struggle—I was out.

I staggered out of that wall and into the cave on shaking legs. Terrified. That was the worst thing I had *ever* had to do.

And it was dark inside the cave. Much too dark to see.

I fumbled in my pocket. The head torch—the head torch the Clodd gave me! I could use that! I put the head torch on, fast as I could.

A beam of light shone out—and there was Bill.

Sprawled on the sand, out cold. With a big lump on his head, and a chunk of rock right beside him.

I ran over. Then looked around, panicking more and more and MORE. I had to get us out of here, boggle both of us out through that wall...

No.

No, no, NO.

Just the thought was making my whole body start shaking. It was *impossible*. I knew it was. Remembering that last wall, how hard it was. And now this... Wallboggling with Bill...

I couldn't do it. I could NOT do it.

But I had to. We couldn't stay here. We *couldn't*.

Wallboggling with Bill was the ONLY choice. And I had to TRY.

But I couldn't lift him. I heaved and heaved—but I could NOT lift him. Not while he was out cold. It was like lifting three Bills, not one.

'Bill,' I said, panicking more. 'Wake up! WAKE UP! You *have* to!'

But Bill didn't.

Then I heard a sound. A splashing sound. The sound of the first waves swooshing up to the cave entrance.

I turned and I stared—as water came creeping into the cave.

NO.

It was here. The sea was *here*. Already. Coming in faster, MUCH faster than I ever thought it would.

Every bit of me trembled. If the sea was here, already up to the cave, then I was too late.

Even if I *could* lift Bill, even if I *could* boggle my way through the wall with him, we wouldn't make it. Wouldn't be fast enough. Not to get through the water. Not to get up over the rocks.

The moment to get out with Bill...

It was GONE.

**34**

'Bill,' I said, crouching beside him, terrified. 'Bill! You *have* to wake up. You HAVE to!'

But Bill just lay there, silent and still.

I felt alone. So *so* alone. Trapped here, in the cave— with water lapping over the sand. Creeping across the cave towards me and Bill.

'Bill,' I said, shaking his shoulders. 'BILL! Wake up. *Please* wake UP!'

But Bill didn't stir.

I felt panic. What to do? What *could* I do?

Then—AT LAST—Bill gave a groan.

Relief surged through me. 'Bill!' I said. 'You're AWAKE!'

Bill opened his eyes. Stared up at me, a bit dazed, a bit dopey... Then he tried to scowl.

'*Stop* the scowling,' I said, grabbing his shoulders. 'Because right now—you and me are in a SERIOUSLY TRICKY situation!'

Bill stared more at me. 'We are?' he said, still dazed.

'Look around you,' I said, half-dragging him up, so he was sitting.

Bill *did* look around him, with a baffled sort of look on his face. 'The cave...' he said. 'WHY are we here in the cave?'

Then he groaned. 'My head...' he said. 'It hurts... But... what *happened*? There was noise—lots of noise... and then...'

He went pale. 'Oh,' he said.

He stared at the blocked cave entrance. Stared at the water creeping towards us. Stared at me...

The dazed look vanished off his face. He grabbed my arm. 'Ned, we're *trapped*!' he said, panicking. 'Here, in this cave! And the water—it's rising...'

'Yes,' I said, jumping to my feet—trying to sound a *lot* more confident than I felt. 'And that is why we have to FIND that wreckers' tunnel. And *fast*!'

The wreckers' tunnel...

It was our ONLY hope.

Last time we looked we didn't look hard enough. We missed something, we *must* have. Some clue to where it was.

Well—this time we were NOT missing anything. This time we were going to *find* it. We WERE.

But terrified thoughts whirled around in my brain. Could we find it? A tunnel no one had found for hundreds of years? Here, in the dark, with just the light from my head torch? And suppose it wasn't even *here* to find? It was a rumour, but suppose it wasn't *true*?

No. No, no, *no*. It *was* here. It HAD to be.

So we got searching. Me, Bill, both of us—searching desperately. Fast as we could, but carefully. Checking, then double-checking, along EVERY wall of that cave. Tapping, knocking, feeling along it, peering right up at it. Checking every line, every striation, every nook, every cranny. Searching and searching for the tunnel— that hidden tunnel.

But there was no sign of it. No sign of it *anywhere*.

'The other caves!' I said, running towards the first small cave. 'We'll try these. It HAS to be in one of these!'

But I was scared. SO scared. Because now the water was creeping up over our ankles. Spilling into the caves, faster and faster.

'I'm cold,' said Bill, teeth chattering as he followed me. 'So cold.'

Then he grabbed my arm. *'We're* not going to find

it, Ned,' he said, staring at me, terror in his eyes, his whole body trembling. 'We're not.'

'We ARE!' I said. And I splashed on through the water. Checking and checking, all along the wall.

On and on and on we both searched. Checking in one... two... three of the smaller caves. Searching as hard as we could, wall after wall.

But there was STILL no sign of it.

And the water came creeping, higher and higher— now almost up to our knees...

One final cave. That was all that was left. Just one final cave. One last chance.

If the tunnel wasn't in here, there was nothing we could do.

NOTHING.

'This is it,' said Bill, teeth chattering more, face ghostly pale. 'But, Ned... Suppose it's not here? Suppose it doesn't *exist*!'

'It *will* be here,' I said, shivering with cold, with terror—as the water came creeping up over my knees. 'It WILL.'

I stared. I stared and I stared and I STARED at that cave wall, searching along it. Desperate—for signs, for clues, for anything. *Anything.*

'But, Ned... suppose it's *not* here?' said Bill, clinging on to my arm now. 'Suppose it's NOT? Then what? WHAT?'

I didn't answer. Not because there WAS no answer—but because of the *wall*.

It was the striations. The lines. There were so *many* of them. Lines everywhere. Lines up, lines down, lines across the rocks.

But those lines... Something wasn't, well—quite *right* about them.

Was it that they seemed a bit less... haphazard? A bit less... natural? A bit more... planned?

A bit more MAN-MADE?

I felt the first flutterings of something inside. Flutterings of *hope*.

Because it was VERY tricky to spot—but those lines... did some of them form an outline? A faint panel shape? Cleverly disguised—but as tall as me, and as wide as three of me...

The longer I stared the more I began to be sure.

'Bill,' I said. 'Look!'

Then I followed the lines with my finger—across, and down. 'See?' I said. 'This bit of wall—I think it could be *false*!'

Yes.

Now I was sure. Sure as sure as SURE.

It *was* a false wall. It WAS. Slotted into place to hide something *behind* it...

Like a TUNNEL.

**35**

We could NOT shift it. We tried *everything*. Pushing at it. Pressing at it. Heaving at it.

Nothing worked. That wall was NOT budging. It was wedged tight shut, and had been for hundreds of years.

And now time was RUNNING OUT. We *had* to get out of here. Had to get away from the sea swirling into the caves, swirling all around us, swirling up our legs. Had to get into that tunnel, and make our way up—up and up and UP.

I stared at the wall, at the stupid *stupid* wall. What was wrong with it? Why was there no way to move it. WHY?

'We're *trapped*, Ned,' said Bill beside me, a sob in his voice. 'TRAPPED.'

And we were.

I think that moment will stay with me for ever. Standing

there, water swirling up my legs, knowing we were trapped. Knowing what I had to do...

To wallboggle my way into the tunnel... With BILL.

Bill was as terrified as I was when I told him. He started shaking his head, trembling and shivering.

'No, no, no, NO,' he said, teeth clacking hard as he spoke. 'Not the wallboggling thing. Not THAT.'

'We have NO choice,' I said. 'None.'

Then I grabbed his shoulders. 'Bill—I wallboggled with a *chicken*,' I said. 'With Esmerelda. She was OK. So you will be too.'

I did my best to sound sure of myself—but Bill was NOT fooled. He could see how terrified I was. More terrified than I had EVER been.

He shook his head even more. 'A chicken?' he said. '*Look* at me, Ned! I am about as big as SEVEN—maybe EIGHT—chickens! And wallboggling with a chicken does *not* mean you can wallboggle with a BOY!'

He shook his head more. 'I am absolutely NOT going,' he said. 'You won't be able to do it. Then we'll *both* get stuck. So... *you* go through. Get help.'

He started nodding. 'Yes,' he said, teeth clacking even harder. 'That's the best plan. Definitely. Do THAT, Ned. Do it now. Quick!'

But now it was me who was shaking my head. 'There's no time,' I said. 'NONE!'

'Then at least you'll be safe,' said Bill—his chin jutting out and a fat tear rolling out of each eye.

I shook Bill by the shoulders. 'Bill,' I said. 'STOP trying to be a hero!'

Bill gulped. 'You were a hero first,' he said. 'Coming back through the wall to help me. I think it's only FAIR you save yourself.'

Then another fat tear rolled out of each eye. Because now the water was swirling right up to our middles.

'I'm not actually trying to be a hero,' he said, in a small voice. 'It's just the wallboggling—I'm terrified.'

'Bill,' I replied. 'So am I. But I wallboggled in to get you—and I am NOT leaving you here while I wallboggle out on my own. We're going together. And that is *that*!'

Then I took off my belt—a stretchy one—and pulled it to its very longest. 'Here,' I said. 'We'll put it round both of us.'

Bill nodded. 'Do it quickly,' he said, shutting his eyes tight. 'Just do it quickly.'

My hands were trembling as I did up the belt, me in front, Bill behind.

Then I stood there, trying to keep as calm as I could. Trying to control the panicky feelings shuddering right through me.

*You have to do this!* I told myself. *You HAVE to!*

Then I stared at the wall. Focused.

I stared and I stared and I stared. Focused and focused...

It was no good. Nothing happened. Not a *thing*. I could NOT block out those thoughts. Those terrifying thoughts about wallboggling.

I undid the belt and turned around, then looked at Bill.

'I can't do it,' I said—panicking more than I EVER thought possible. 'The wallboggling—it's been getting harder. I think, maybe, it just won't *work.* I can't do it. Can't make it happen. Not any more.'

I stood, shivering, water swirling all around us, higher still. Was it gone? Was my wallboggling really REALLY gone?

But Bill... something was happening to him. He was staring at me. Staring and staring, like he was coming to some sort of *decision.*

Then he stood up straighter. And—somehow—the panic left his eyes. He got a look on his face, a determined sort of look...

He got me by both shoulders. Stared straight into my eyes.

'Know what *I* think, Ned?' he said firmly. 'I think you CAN do it!'

'You do?' I said, teeth chattering.

'Most DEFINITELY,' Bill said, even more firmly. 'No doubt about it.'

He stared more. Held my shoulders harder. 'Who has the biggest stubborn streak of any kid in the universe?' he said. '*You*, Ned! And that wall is NOT going to defeat you. I don't think that wall has a CHANCE against you.'

'You don't?' I said, still shivering.

'No,' said Bill, staring harder. 'And I also think this. That if *any* kid can manage to wallboggle—even with me, who is probably *eight times bigger* than a chicken—it is YOU, Ned! Edward Harrison Arkle-Smith. Wallboggler SUPREME. So GO for it! Right NOW!'

**36**

Something *changed* inside me. Knowing that Bill—the friend I believed I had lost for ever—thought I could DO this.

Because, if Bill thought I could, then I *would* do this. I was NOT letting Bill down.

No. Not ever again.

So, once more, I did up the belt. I took a deep breath. Then I stared at the wall, and focused.

I could do this. I *could*. *Don't think about it*, I told myself. *Just DO it. You can do it. You* can*!*

Because—maybe my wallboggling *was* going, the way my anger with walls was going. But right here, right now—I WAS angry.

I was *sizzling* with anger. With FURY. Fury at the wall. At THIS wall.

Me and Bill were here, trapped, water surging all around us—in the DEADLIEST PERIL I could possibly imagine. And that wall was *not* going to stop us getting out of here. It was NOT.

Because on the other side of that wall was the tunnel, and safety. On the other side of that wall were all the people I loved, the people I wanted to see.

My family.

And there was only one thing in my way. That WALL.

So I stood, and I stared—and I *sizzled*.

'I hate you, wall!' I said, and my eyes felt burning hot now. 'Hate you, *hate* you, HATE you! Because you are IN MY WAY!'

Then it happened. That feeling, whooshing right through me. That blazing, sizzling feeling. Like a gigantic surge of POWER, of ENERGY...

Whoosh! Me and Bill—we *shot* through that wall. *Tumbled* through that wall. Straight into the secret wreckers' tunnel.

And as I lay there, sprawled on the tunnel floor, I knew two things for sure.

First—that was my BEST, most MAGNIFICENT wallboggle *ever*...

And second—it was also my LAST.

I can't remember who started the silly dancing on the clifftop—me or Bill. But one of us did.

Because the clifftop was where the tunnel came out. Up and up it wound and, at the very top, was a rotting trapdoor. We broke our way through it, and climbed out.

And there we were. High up on the cliffs, in the far corner of a field. A field I knew well, the very first field by the footpath—right near Ivy Lodge. With the trapdoor all hidden behind shrubs and gorse.

That's when the silly dancing started. Both of us, flinging ourselves about, whooping and cheering. Taking deep breaths of that wet windy air. Not caring that we were both soaked through.

*So* so happy to be out. To be SAFE.

Then we both collapsed, in a heap. And Bill turned to me, shivering and dripping—but also thinking. Hard.

'Ned,' he said. 'I should NOT have jumped on your

garbage gobbler. But then, you should NOT have set the trap.'

Then he beamed the Bill-beam. 'Which makes us equals,' he said.

'Equals,' I said, beaming back.

But now a frown crossed Bill's face. 'Except...' he said, slowly, 'you have now saved my life not once, but TWICE. So *are* we actually equals?'

'We ARE,' I said firmly. 'Because that first time—all I did was push you out of the way, so that wasn't saving your life, not really. And the second time—well, I was just doing what friends do. They look out for each other. You'd do the same for me.'

That did it.

The beam was back on Bill's face. We did our secret seven-part handshake—and that was it. Things were all right with me and Bill.

Yes. We were starting over. And this time, I would NOT mess up.

I hoped...

Bill got a Highly Commended certificate for his starfish costume on BayDay. And he has had no more trouble with Snapper...

*No one* has trouble with Snapper. Not any more.

Because the Hulk is *still* being nice to him. And it's become a sort of habit. Just like the kids in the legend.

'He forgets to behave now and then,' Snapper told me. 'But I remind him about the poltergeist, and that shuts him up.'

Snapper told me that at drum practice—because me and him are both learning drums. And he says it's an honour drumming with a kid who was once a wallboggler. Also that, if he gets a magic skill, he wants to turn into a fish any time he likes.

We're not really friends again, not yet. But we're getting there.

Slowly.


The Clodd CONTINUES to get on my nerves. Latest thing—she hopped over the wall when I was out in the front garden, and handed me a table tennis bat. 'Time for your audition,' she said.

'Audition?' I said.

'To see if you're good enough to be my partner,' she said.

I ask you...

Still, I'm stuck with her. Not only for table tennis—which we DO plan to win, by the way, like we won for our octopus costume on BayDay—but living next door.

And it's not just the Clodd next door.

Ruby has joined her.

Turns out the Clodd's mum and dad decided that sharing the Clodd and Ruby needed UNdeciding.

Because Ruby sobbed herself to sleep every night she was apart from the Clodd. And she refused to do sums or writing in school, just drew pictures of the Clodd all day. Then, soon as she got home from school, she made all her teddies and dollies draw pictures of the Clodd...

As for the Clodd, her mum found her sleepwalking one night. Trying to unlock the front door, dreaming she was off to catch a train to see Ruby...

So now Ruby—keen elf-hunter, and Isabel's new best friend—lives with the Clodd. And the Clodd and Ruby visit their dad lots of weekends and holidays.

'It's not the family we once were,' the Clodd told me. 'But it's better than before.'

And I knew exactly what she meant.

It's like me and the walls. Because I know now. Those walls, they ARE there to keep my family together. A way to keep us—Dad, Mum, the sisters, and me—all together, all under one roof.

Together in a new way. Not my *chosen* way, but the best way possible.

As for my wallboggling skill—it's gone, at least for now. Maybe it'll be back, maybe not. I don't know.

And I *still* don't know what it was.

Was it science? Was it magic? Was Grace right— that Matilda Arkle had a magic gene she passed on to me?

I have no idea, but it doesn't matter. Not one bit.

Because wallboggling came along just when I needed it. It helped me sort things out, and make things better—with my friends, with my family, with the walls...

And that's ALL I really need to know.

## About the Author

Emma Fischel grew up in the Kent countryside, the middle child of five. She spent many years in London but is now back in Kent. Her favourite wall curves in waves along the side of an orchard near her house, and is called a crinkle-crankle wall. If Emma is ever offered a superpower, being able to teleport between Kent and London would be very handy.

## A Word from the Author

Thank you to the wonderful team at OUP. Special thanks to Kathy Webb, eagle-eyed editor, for nagging me so charmingly until *Walls* became the best book I could make it. Also thanks to Sarah Darby for her dazzlingly stylish orange cover.

And to my agent, Julia Churchill, and to Sarah Molloy who first spotted a spark of something in my writing—many, many thanks.

NOT READY
TO FINISH YET?

TURN THE PAGE FOR
SOME GREAT *WALLS*
ACTIVITIES AND FUN . . .

TURN THE PAGE

# QUIZ

Have a go at this quiz.

Choose your answers from **a**, **b**, or **c**.

(One of the questions has two answers!)

1. **What gives Ned the power to wallboggle?**
   - **a.** Sizzling anger
   - **b.** An iron fist
   - **c.** A spell he finds in an old book

2. **What gave Ned such a frightening experience that he needs to do things his way and be in control?**
   - **a.** A ghost
   - **b.** Rice pudding
   - **c.** Custard

3. **What does Ned do to help himself feel more in control of things?**
   - **a.** Eat a favourite meal
   - **b.** Read a favourite book
   - **c.** Sort all his books and pencils into order

4. **In the summer holidays Ned's friend Bill has made new friends and gone bouldering. What is bouldering?**
   - **a.** Making a beach sculpture with piles of rocks
   - **b.** Building a stone wall
   - **c.** A form of climbing without using ropes

**5.** **What is Ned's favourite animal?**

   **a.** An elephant

   **b.** A lemur

   **c.** A cat

**6.** **Why is Ned's next-door neighbour Maddie on the phone a lot?**

   **a.** She's worried about her grandmother

   **b.** She's worried about her little sister

   **c.** She has a lot of friends

**7.** **What did Matilda Arkle, Ned's ancestor, want to do in her life?**

   **a.** Build a house by the sea and have adventures

   **b.** Marry a rich man and have lots of children

   **c.** Stay at home and write books

**8.** **Who were Morwenna and Drummond Moraggon?**

   **a.** Ned's friends when he was young

   **b.** Twins who were mean to each other and were haunted by the Craggelton poltergeist

   **c.** Characters in a story book

**9.** **How does Ned do a good deed for his sister Grace when George, her boyfriend, dumps her?**

    **a.** He wallboggles into George's room and frightens him

    **b.** He wallboggles into George's room and covers things with slime and itching powder

    **c.** He challenges George to a fight

**10.** **Who is Snapper?**

    **a.** A photographer from a newspaper

    **b.** Someone who used to be Ned's friend

    **c.** The Hulk's stepbrother

**11.** **What danger does Ned save Bill from?**

    **a.** Being trapped in a cave by the rising tide

    **b.** Falling from a cliff

    **c.** Being crushed by a collapsing wall

**12.** **What does Ned realize about the walls in his house?**

    **a.** They are very thin

    **b.** They wobble

    **c.** They are keeping his family together

# NICKNAMES

**What are the real names of these characters in *Walls*?**

- Snapper
- The Clodd
- The Great Beauty

**What nicknames do you think Ned could give to these book characters?**

**For example, Harry Potter could be *The Wizard*.**

- Matilda
- Frodo
- Paddington
- Peter Pan
- Pinocchio
- Cinderella

# LISTS

**Why do you think Ned likes making lists?**

- *'Secret Sleuth', number one of my top ten favourite books. (p19)*
  What are your top ten favourite books?
- *Lemurs are number one of my top twenty-five best animals. (p43)*
  What are your top ten favourite animals?
  And did you know that in French the words *le mur* mean 'the wall'?

Get a notebook and start making and collecting your own lists! Here are some you might want to include: 'My five worst dinners'; 'My ten best things to do'; 'Ten reasons why I like my family'.

# CUSTARDOPHOBIA!

A phobia is an extreme fear of something. Here are the names of some phobias which many people have. Their descriptions have been muddled up—see if you can match each phobia to its correct description.

| PHOBIA | DESCRIPTION |
| --- | --- |
| 1. Agoraphobia | a. Fear of spiders |
| 2. Ornithophobia | b. Fear of being enclosed in small spaces |
| 3. Claustrophobia | c. Fear of dentists |
| 4. Arachnophobia | d. Fear of sleep |
| 5. Somniphobia | e. Fear of open spaces |
| 6. Zoophobia | f. Fear of numbers |
| 7. Dentophobia | g. Fear of birds |
| 8. Arithmophobia | h. Fear of animals |

# WALLS—MAKE ONE HOUSE INTO TWO!

Here is a floor plan of the
ground floor of a house.

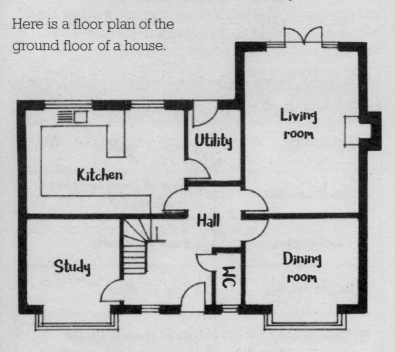

Living
room

Utility

Kitchen

Hall

Study

WC

Dining
room

Have a go at drawing a floor plan of your house—
downstairs, upstairs, or both.

Imagine you are one of Ned's parents and you are trying
to divide the house into two parts. Can you find a way
of doing this with your house? Where might you put in a
wall, or walls?
If it looks too difficult to do this with your house, have a go
at dividing up the ground floor of the house in the plan
above.

# THINGS TO THINK ABOUT . . .

- How did you feel when reading this book? And how did you feel when you'd finished it?

- Which parts of the story do you remember most?

- Was there anything that took you by surprise?

- Who was your favourite character in the book? Why? And who was your least favourite?

- What kind of book did you think it was going to be?

- What would you say about this book if you were telling someone about what you've just read?

- At the end of the book did you feel as if you'd been there in the story, too?

- How do you feel about Ned, the main character? What would you think about him if you met him in real life? Would you like to be friends with him?

- Can you think of more stories or films where a character can walk through walls? Maybe to another world or another dimension?

- What similarities do you see in Ned and Matilda Arkle, Ned's ancestor, and what do you think are the reasons for their behaviour?

- What superpower would you like to have?
  Ned can wallboggle, Emma Fischel, the author of *Walls*, wants to be able to teleport. The Clodd would choose flying, and Snapper wishes he could turn into a fish.

  - What would you do with your chosen superpower?

  - And what would you do if your superpower was wallboggling, like Ned's?

- Your secret spot—and your favourite place:
  Ned's secret spot is on the riverbank, over the wall at the bottom of the Ivy Lodge garden.

  - What's your secret place to sit and think?

  - What's your favourite place to be in your house?

# ANSWERS

**Quiz:**
1. (a)
2. (c)
3. (c)
4. (c)
5. (b)
6. (b)
7. (a)
8. (b)
9. (b)
10. (b) and (c)
11. (a)
12. (c)

**Phobias:**
1. (e)
2. (g)
3. (b)
4. (a)
5. (d)
6. (h)
7. (c)
8. (f)

- **Nicknames:**
- Samuel is Snapper
- Maddie is The Clodd
- Grace is The Great Beauty

# Ready for more great stories?

## Try one of these...

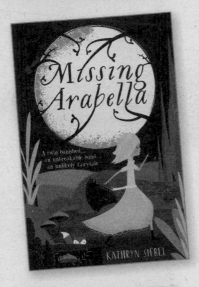